FIRST OF JULES

This book is a work of fiction. Names, character, places, and incidents are the product of the author's imagination or are used fictitiously. Any resemblance to actual events, locales, or persons, living or dead, is coincidental.

First Printing, 2015

ISBN-10: 0996327800

ISBN-13: 978-0-9963278-0-0

Bad Day Publication
391 Muncy Street
Lindenhurst, NY 11757

www.BaddayPublication.com

Printed in the United States of America

Gasch Printing
1780 Crossroads Drive
Odenton, MD 21113

Jacket design by Nancy Batra and Jamee Mascia

ALSO BY GENE HILGREEN

FIRST OF

JULES

GENE HILGREEN

For my granddaughter Jules

1

Isla Grand Beach Resort
South Padre Island, Texas
Sunday Night March 31st

A salty gust ripped across the beach and through the crowd as he worked his way past the throng of dancing Phish worshippers and spring breakers. Tony's perfectly coiffed hair fell across his forehead—that disturbed him. On the prowl, his eyes zigzagged back and forth, he needed to quench his thirst and needs. He wasn't just looking for sex; he needed to support his lifestyle—he siphoned off the rich. The outcome all depended on the victim.

Tony Labarbera, a high school dropout, hailed from Odessa, Texas a booming town along the southwestern edge of the Llano Estacado in West Texas. He moved to Houston at sixteen, and found a job with a cleaning company. With his dashing good looks and charm, he soon became popular among the rich, unhappy, trophy wives and cougar population of Houston—those who were more interested in sexual relations than having their pools or carpets cleaned.

Cleaning, or any kind of work in general, was not Tony's strong suit, and he soon became arm candy for his richest customers. He would help himself to jewelry, cash, and anything lying around their mansions that he could sell on the quick—this, of course, was on top of the four-hundred dollars a night, plus expenses, he demanded for his services.

Tony's greed caught up to him when he lifted a pearl and diamond necklace valued at over one hundred thousand dollars. The woman threatened to call the cops, and Tony returned the necklace.

A week later, her gardener found her floating—face down dead—in her pool. An empty bottle of Cristal Brut champagne sat on a table by her lounger, another empty bottle and a fluted glass floated nearby her in the pool. Toxicology screens had her blood level at .282. With the lack of any other evidence, the authorities labeled the death an accident. It wasn't the first time Tony got away with murder—and it wouldn't be the last.

Tony came across an ad for an up-and-coming cleaning company in Houston looking to expand its operations on South Padre Island. Tony thought, *why not*, rich women, living on the beach, and with Mexico minutes away, it would be a blast. He packed his meager belongs and left town.

The owner of the cleaning company eyed Tony up and down. Dressed in jeans and a tight T-shirt that emphasized his physique—the owner was impressed, and offered him fifteen dollars-an-hour. Tony tried to pour on his charm, but the fifty year-old retired Marine didn't bite. Tony would have to make his spending money the old fashion way: stealing it. He took the offer.

The pit in front of the stage was well lit, and Tony watched as a group of young girls danced. *Interesting, but no money there*, he thought. He walked past them, and stopped to looked back, making note of where they were in the pit. He'd check back if nothing else rang his bell. As it was, he hadn't banged a young chick in over a week. He continued on, and as he drew to the edge of the crowd he found his marks—two hotties dressed to the nines. Their outfits and jewelry said it all: money, money, honey.

As he zeroed in on them, a tall blond hair kid swooped in from nowhere. He grabbed the super sexy brunette and started dancing with her. The equally sexy stunner with the long blonde hair huffed, and locked her arms under her impressive breasts. She turned away from the two, and scanned the crowd for someone to dance with. All around her, piss drunk college boys acted like asses. She turned back toward her friends, and did a double take, for coming her way was her prince charming.

A master of manipulation, and dressed—killer casual—Tony turned on the charm as he tucked his stolen little white Chihuahua under his arm. He ran a hand through his slightly long yet stylish dark hair to place the locks back in place. Without missing a beat, he approached the third wheel. "Tony at your service. Would you care to dance?"

The smile that spread across the hot chick's face as her ample breasts heaved in and out told Tony the answer would be yes.

One look into his dark brown sparkling eyes, and the little Chihuahua sealed the deal. "Gunther's loss," she said, while flipping her hair. "Sure, Tony, I'd love to dance. My name is Sandy."

Tony set down the Chihuahua—that was soon forgotten, and danced her off from ear shot of the other two. After the set, he asked. "Would you care for a drink?"

"Sure, but I'd prefer a little snow . . . if you catch my drift."

Tony feigned a shy look, then asked. "Are you a cop?"

Sandy let out one of those giggles that girls make when asked a stupid question. "No, silly," she said, as she ran her perfectly manicured fingers across Tony's chest.

Tony stared at the other couple, who were now in a passionate kiss. "I know a place where it gets a little chilly."

Sandy caught his meaning and followed his stare. "Screw them," she said, and then giggled again. "Let's get out of here."

Tony had removed the cleaning equipment from the van before he left his trailer, and had thrown an over-sized bean bag lounger in the back. And after a quick stop at the drive through car wash for a vacuum, he figured the van was perfect for a night of debauchery. And it was, for he quickly laid out a couple of lines of his Special K concoction as soon as they got inside. After a couple of minutes of foreplay on the bean bag, and a few more lines of coke, Sandy was in buzzville. He had no problem convincing her to leave for his hidey-hole in the dunes near the Island Adventure Park.

When they arrived, Sandy wanted more cocaine— Tony wanted sex.

They both got their way.

He started out with foreplay, and when Sandy began to moan louder—the groping got rougher. Tony pulled down her skirt and ripped off her panties. While removing her skin tight top it got caught around her neck.

"Oh yeah baby," yelled Sandy. "I like it rough! Squeeze my neck some more!"

Tony complied, and squeezed harder—unaware of the gagging sound that was escaping her lips. His persona changed. He had been here before, and his hands came

5

together, fingers interlocked, his grip tightened around the nape of her long, neck.

Sandy's head flopped to the side.

Tony slapped her cheeks several times, but didn't receive a reaction. The sweat pouring down his cheeks was not from nervousness; this wasn't the first one he lost to asphyxiation. He gathered her clothes, and inspected his hideout for any traces of the girl. Satisfied that nothing was left behind, he threw her over his shoulders, and carried her south along the bayside shoreline. A couple of hundred feet later, he found a mass of secluded dunes, and unceremoniously dropped her on the sand.

He looked around for driftwood, or anything he could dig with, but found nothing. Tony began shoveling with his bare hands until he was satisfied with the depth of the grave. He kicked her in and spent the next ten minutes covering her up.

Darkness crept along the dunes as a cloud layer passed across the moon. Tony believed the body was hidden, but gave a few more deep sweeping kicks of sand with his foot to be sure. He continued sweeping his feet across his retreating footsteps, and only stopped when he reached the wet packed shoreline. He never looked back as he made his way back to his hide-out.

In her grave, Sandy coughed one last time.

Tony never heard her—he'd left her for dead.

Safely in his van he drove south to his trailer park.

A lone figure emerged from the shadows of the dunes, less than fifty feet from Tony's secluded playground. This individual's curiosity had led to Tony's little hideaway on numerous occasions, and was certain it wouldn't be the last. His lust for preying on rich women, plying them with drugs, and having his way with them piqued this person's interest.

The mysterious stalker also had an interest with the woman he had chosen for this particular tryst. The lone figure had special plans for Tony, he made too many mistakes, and this would play perfectly into the individual's own plans.

Out of sheer happenstance, the individual took a boat to Louie's that night. Louie's charged a fifty dollar docking fee that would be deducted from their food and bar bill to cover the losses of people who brought their own booze. The lone figure was not concerned in the least, and ate the fifty dollar loss. The mysterious person's interest was captivated solely by Tony and the woman he'd left with.

Travelling by boat and knowing Tony's routine, the person had plenty of time to hide the boat and witness the whole encounter. The shadowy figure waited for Tony to leave, and watched as the rear lights of his van disappeared in the night, and then retraced Tony's movements back to the spot where the body was buried.

Not such a good job of concealment, the figure thought. Glints of moonlight reflected perfectly off the sand, revealing strands of long golden blonde hair which blew in the wind. Twin snaps of rubber were heard as the mystery person tugged and stretched the gloves into a more comfortable position. The figure dug up the body—made certain she was dead, wrapped the body and the clothes into a heavy plastic tarp-like bag, and then hefted the body to the awaiting boat.

With the body safely tucked away in the lower level cabin in an ice chest, to be disposed of at a later date. The figure sailed the boat back to the docks at South Padre Island Fishing, secured the boat lines, and headed home.

2

Colorado Springs, Colorado
Saturday March 23rd

Jules Spenser climbed the steps onto the raised floor exercise spring platform. "Clear the mechanism," she whispered to herself.

Nothing happened.

The screams of excited fans echoed throughout the gymnasium, as well as through her ears which unnerved her a bit. "Clear the mechanism," she said aloud as she stepped onto the mat. The sounds became muffled in the background as her focus turned to the mathematical calculations of the boundary line, and routine. All she saw was the first tumbling pass unfold across the mat.

Jules turned toward the judges, and struck her pose. The head judge nodded. She raised her right arm straight up. The music started, she began with two steps, and a powerful leap.

She didn't hear the roar of the crowd when Alena scored a 16.146 average for her two vaults. However, as she prepared for her final tumbling pass by performing a combination spin into a backward Valdez and leg split, she glanced up as Alena's score posted on the board. A brief smile appeared on her face as she lowered her chest to the floor—finishing her Japanese split. Time seemed to stop in the nanosecond when she saw the score. Thoughts flashed through Jules' mind. Then the smile vanished. She also calculated that she needed to average a 15.6 on floor to make the top three in all-around.

She raised her hands over her head, and drew in a deep breath. She slowly released it, and leapt into her final tumbling pass. With a matchless step in her dance—like a shimmering nymph traveling the back of the wind, her moves blurred into one.

She had several major deductions that she could count, but the crowd didn't care and screamed her name.

When the judges posted her final score of 15.2, the crowd's cheers turned into boos. Jules acknowledged their concern with a wave, but knew she messed up.

The top twenty-four gymnasts from national qualifications were assigned to one of four groups by their national ranking. Each group performed on one of four different apparatus at the same time—balance beam, uneven bars, floor exercise, and the vault.

The top three scorers in all-around—the total of all four events—were a lock to make Team USA, and represent the United States of America at the World Championships. Five additional gymnasts would be added by the National Selection Committee. Ranked nineteenth in the country, and seated in the fourth and final group was Jules. Her chances of making the team were slim. Her nemesis Alena Shenkova—the odds-on favorite to take the top spot—was seated first in Group One.

The first three rotations were complete, and the darling of USA, fifteen year old Alena was four-tenths of a point ahead of the field in the all-around competition.

Jules caught an edge and fell off the balance beam, and she blew the landing on her dismount from the uneven bars. Her 15.2 on floor exercise earned her a bronze medal, and moved her up to twelfth place, but she was still 1.2 points behind the leader, and .8 out of third place in all-around. The vault was her event to make a difference.

Without missing a beat she walked toward the competitor's seating area with a swagger in her gait. "Take that Alena," she said, as Alena Shenkova stole a quick glance before turning away. Her face and clenched jaw said it all. Jules saw the pride of USA appeared nervous.

You better sweat, thought Jules. *This is my event, my last hurrah, and you better bring it.*

Jules would turn seventeen in three weeks; there would be no World Championships or Olympics for her. She had decided this was her last meet, and only a handful of people knew this fact. She would announce her retirement from gymnastics at a later date—or not—she always left her options open.

That's how Jules rolled.

Her internship at the research center would tax her to the max, and leave little time for anything else. Jules believed she wouldn't have the time or stamina on top of her work load to give the sport she loved the required training. However, she could walk away proud, and she thought, *go big or go home.*

"You gotta risk it to get the biscuit," Jules whispered, as she thought of Grandpa Buck watching from the stands. She knew it was his favorite motto, and a smile crossed her face.

Meanwhile, Buck Davidssen sat half way up in the stands. He had the perfect view for the next and final event for Jules—the vault. At fifty-three, the six foot, one-hundred ninety pound grandfather, sporting a blondish grey flat top appeared every bit the gymnast and Marine he was years ago. He watched as his only granddaughter, Jules Spenser, paced back and forth in front of the competitors bench.

He knew her routines by heart, and knew she was looking for her *mechanism*.

Lithe yet powerful, Jules displayed the grace of a ballerina with the burst of speed of a sprinter. She was still a baby in Buck's mind, but even he had to admit that she had become a young woman. At five foot eight, she was considered tall for her sport, and it affected her floor exercise routine where, because of her size, she ate up yardage incredibly fast. She had to limit her stride after each tumbling pass just to stay in bounds.

Her blonde hair was tied in a fashionable bun and her cobalt blue eyes, like her mother and grandfather, exuded confidence. When she locked eyes with an opponent, she was all business.

Buck donned his advanced ear mic so he could hear the TV announcers over the noise in the gymnasium. His R-CAT, an advanced smartphone developed by his company—*The Corporation*—locked on the FOX Sports channel.

"Jules is up next," he said to Anna and his daughter Jax.

Anna with her thick Russian accent blurted, "*Vat?*"

Jax, who adored Anna, was sitting just below them and laughed out loud. She leaned back against Bucks knees, and tilted her head backwards. "*Dawlink*, your English is getting so much better."

Anna leaned forward and kissed Jax on the forehead.

On the floor, Jules turned toward the vaulting horse where Alena paced back and forth, and stared her down.

Jules reached into the chalk bin and grabbed a chunk. She bent over to rub it on her feet as the FOX news camera zoomed in on her. Jules caught the back of her neck as it filled the screen on the jumbotron hanging from the ceiling as the cameraman zoomed. There were five colored rings tattooed across the back of her neck—the Olympic rings.

I wonder what Grandpa is thinking.

In the stands, Buck fumbled his R-CAT as the same picture filled his screen. "Will you look at that shit."

Jax hit his knee with her elbow. "Dad!"

"Sorry. When did she get the tattoo?"

Jax gazed at Anna and smiled, then turned toward her father. "Anna and I took her yesterday, Jules wanted to make a statement."

Bucks lips eased into his patented grin, with one corner turned upward. "Well she accomplished that goal."

Jax noted the approval and turned her attention back to the vault.

Jules reached into the chalk bin again and chalked up her hands. She glanced up into the stands toward Buck, her mom, and Anna. With her right arm extended, she pointed at them. Her eyes seemed like they were on fire.

Buck pointed back at her. "She's ready".

"Stick it. . . "

The roar from the crowd echoed through the gymnasium, as Jules race down the mat. In the zone—her mind clear of all distractions—she pushed off the vaulting horse with all the strength her arms could muster. Her body stretched into a perfect layout as she zeroed in on a single point on the ceiling to gain the maximum height.

It didn't take a genius in physics to understand the laws of gravity would draw her upper torso down toward the floor. She waited until her toes pointed at that exact same spot.

Now. . .

Her arms wrapped around her torso as she began her triple twisting Yurchenko—the Maroney—named after American gymnast McKayla Maroney. She prepared for impact with the eight inch thick mat twelve feet beneath her. Only one thought resounded in her mind: *just stick it!*

"Yes!" exploded from her lips with the same force as her vault. Jules nailed the modified Yurchenko, a style that began with a roundoff onto the springboard, and a back handspring onto the vaulting horse.

After a near perfect landing Jules beamed with confidence. She turned toward the judges and bowed. She knew the judges would huddle for a few moments to discuss her vault. Jules was messing with their universe.

Jules locked eyes with Alena as the judges posted a 16.196 for her first vault with a full 6.5 points for difficulty and 9.696 out of ten for execution. Her second vault would rock the world, and Jules' demeanor was as cool as an Aspen breeze. Alena on the other hand had beads of sweat running down her cheeks.

Get ready for my next move, Alena.

Jules' next move stunned the gymnastic community at the qualifiers. The move didn't have an official name because it had never been performed at the World Championships, or the Olympics. The governing body awarded the move a maximum difficulty rating of 7.0, which was the highest ever. They would later name it a 3 1/2 twisting Yurchenko. Jules called it The Spenser—after herself, and she was the only woman in the world with the *biscuits* to throw it.

Jules' ability to clearly process information and formulate solutions to problems at an early age became apparent to her teachers, and supporting cast of family. She skipped grades at an unusual rate, and began taking college level classes by her junior year of high school at the age of twelve.

In addition, the two main women in her grandfather's life Dr. Charlotte 'Char' Vice and Dr. Anna Semyonova labeled her a *Wunderkind*—child prodigy. They also recognized her gift at an early age, and played major roles in Jules' future.

Char was Buck's girlfriend and, at the time, a political powerhouse and DC lawyer who held PhD's in Criminal Justice and Psychiatry. She used her power and influence to enroll Jules in the advanced placement classes for gifted children at Johns Hopkins.

Dr. Anna Semyonova, a world renowned quantum physicist, and a core member of The Corporation, had a unique relationship with both Char and Buck. Arguably the smartest person on the planet, she held PhD's in information technology, and nanobiotechnology, and also held the title of CEO at the South Padre Island Advanced Nanoscience Research Center. As Jules' mentor, she molded her curriculum.

Within three years, Jules would walk away with a Master of Science in Quantum Physics and a minor in computer science. She would begin her internship and PhD program in two weeks at The South Padre Island Advanced Nanoscience Research Center in Texas.

The program combined the three significant disciplines of Nanotechnology: Nanomaterials and Nanoelectronics, Biophysics and Bio-nanotechnology, and Biochemistry and Sensors. Classes were conducted by the Corporation scientists, some of which had left positions at the top universities in the United States.

With the world's largest and fastest cyclotron, and the latest equipment available, enrollment at the facility was limited. The school received forty percent of its funding from the Alphabet Soup community; the CIA, DHS, NSA, and the list went on. Thus, the top candidates were vetted, and US citizenship a requirement. The intelligence sector wanted to insure the recipients joined their forces after graduation.

Jules had two other peculiar traits that augmented her intelligence. Jules had eidetic memory, commonly called photographic or total recall—the ability to recall images, sounds, or objects with great precision. She also acquired the ability to block out everything happening around her—the *Mechanism*—she called it, thereby enabling her to focus her entire moment on the objective at hand. She thought this trait was a gift, while some others saw it her greatest flaw. For they believed it led to her loneliness, black hole like, it could be limitless, dark, and daunting.

Jules walked back to her starting spot, taking in all the excitement around her one last time. The crowd noise, the team camaraderie, and multiple events occurring simultaneously.

Yeah, I'll miss it, but it's time to move on.

As she passed by the cameraman, she pointed at him, winked, and said, "Don't miss this one Dad." The cameraman pulled his head out from his covering and winked back. The man's name was Ramsey Spenser, her father, and he worked the event for the FOX Sports network.

Jules searched the stands near the Vaulting Horse, and found her mom, Jax; Grandpa Buck; and Dr. Anna Semyonova. For the final time that evening, she chalked up her hands and feet, and took position next to the white tape marked with her name next to the mat. She nodded to the head judge to indicate she was ready, and the judge returned the nod.

The roar from the crowd had never ceased and she drank in the enthusiasm. She thought to herself, *this crowd will be witnessing history in the making.*

"Clear the mechanism," she whispered, and the room faded to silence in her world.

She ran down the mat toward the vaulting horse her mind oblivious to the crowd screaming her name, and stomping their feet.

Her strides were measured and exact. She leaped at the designated tape mark. A roundoff onto the springboard, the force of the impact launching her body into the air. With her back to the horse, Jules extended her arms and pushed off the horse. As her body began to fall she pointed he toes at the ceiling, and brought her left hand tight to her chest. Her right hand swathed across her torso, and she began to rotate.

Once.

Twice.

Three and a half twists.

With a blind landing, her toes became her antennae as her feet remained fully arched. They hit the mat on the floor and her heels began to sink in, cushioning her landing. No extra step—a perfect stick.

She bowed to the judges, and then turned to her grandfather and pointed. He pointed back. Jules, her mind relaxed, began to hear the pandemonium in the gym again, as the crowd had indeed witnessed history.

"Seventeen."

"Jules."

Seventeen and Jules echoed off the walls nonstop. The crowd demanded a perfect score.

Confidence and enthusiasm radiated from Jules' face and her gait, as she paraded back to the competitor area. She didn't want to just win, she wanted to shatter the new scoring record. And after the judges huddled for close to three minutes she did.

They had rewarded her vault a 16.733. The crowd booed, even after her combined average score of 16.446 was posted.

Jules ran up into the stands where Grandpa Buck awaited to scoop her up. Tears streamed down her cheeks as Buck embraced her. Jax and Anna joined in the hugging. Her six place finish in all-around would not guarantee her a spot on Team USA.

"At least I won the Vault. It wasn't perfect, but I'll take it." Jules said.

"Listen honey," Buck said. "I didn't see anything wrong with either of your vaults. You stuck 'em both."

Jules smirked, and then said. "Grandpa, the judges just don't like me. Alena's their darling."

"Well, you're my darling."

"Hey, listen up guys, I'm starving," Jules said. "Give me half an hour to say goodbye and clean up, and then I want to go pig out." After an exhausting regiment of exercise and training for the last two years, and with the meet out of the way, all she could think about was food.

"Take your time, honey," Jax said. "We're not going anywhere."

Jules ran off to join the winners and collect her medals. When she returned forty minutes later, she produced the gold medal for vaulting for Grandpa Buck's approval.

He took hold of it, eyeing it proudly. "Thanks Jules," he said. "Hope your kid wins one for you someday."

"Kid? I'm not even dating."

Buck laughed and gave it back. "When I won mine, my dad said the same thing to me."

3

Angel's Landing - Aspen, Colorado
Saturday March 23rd

Jules stared out the window of Anna's Hughes MD-530F—the Rolls-Royce of helicopters—as the forty minute, 110 mile flight from Colorado Springs to Aspen culminated with a flyby of the iconic Maroon Bells. With the sun setting between the twin peaks of Elks Mountain, the view was breathtaking. Blades of light echoed off the mountain resembling fire raining from the sky.

Unlike other mountains in the Rockies that were composed of granite and limestone, the Bells were composed of metamorphic sedimentary mudstone that had hardened into rock over millions of years. The mudstone was responsible for the Bells' distinctive maroon color.

Jules waved to the most photographed mountains in North America. "They are picture perfect, as always." she said and turned her back to the window.

"Selfie," she yelled.

The blades dipped as Anna turned the Hughes toward Buck's estate. She flew over the alpine bistro *Cloud Nine* that sat atop Aspen Highlands. Jules turned and snapped a picture with her smartphone.

In less than an hour, Jules would snap a dozen more selfies with her family while dining at Cloud Nine, with the Maroon Bells as the backdrop.

Anna looped the Hughes once around Grandpa Buck's sprawling estate—*Angel's Landing*—situated on forty acres of heaven at the base of Aspen Highland.

Jules and her parents would be spending the week in Aspen skiing before jetting off to South Padre Island— SPI to the locals—for the end of spring break.

SPI claimed less than one-thousand full time citizens. A quarter of them worked for the Advance Nanoscience Research Center controlled by Grandpa's, *The Corporation*.

Jules smiled as she tucked one of the brochures back in the seat pocket. On the cover it stated: Nothing beats the sunrise and sunset on SPI—PERIOD.

Spring Break, which normally drew twenty to thirty thousand high school and college kids, ran the month of

March on SPI. This year it would extend at least three more days with Phish performing on April Fools' Day.

Jules, as-well-as her mom and dad were *Phish Phreaks.* Jax and Ramsey would stay until the sixth of April to celebrate Jules' seventeenth birthday in style.

Angel's Landing had two heliports—one for guests with a walkway to the main entrance, and the second for access to Buck's corporate headquarters. It sat protected by a ten foot high stone wall fortress, with a manned gated Porte-cochere providing the only access for vehicles.

Jules waved to the very large man wearing a black beret tipped at the perfect military angle. "Is that Sarge?" she asked, as the man waved back.

"The one and only," said Buck. Ron 'Sarge' Porter was the head of security at Angel's Landing, and a long time friend of Bucks'.

The Hughes was met by Jack Mameli. He stood at a cool six-foot-one and had a jarhead haircut that could land a plane, and rippling muscles that stretched the US Marine Corp Snake-eater shirt he wore to its max. Jack was Buck's right-hand man, and served under him in the Corps.

"How was the trip Cap'n?" Jack said, as he gave Buck their secret Marine Corps handshake.

"Could have been better," returned Jules."

Jules ran into Jack's waiting arms, and got a kiss on the top of her head. "I won the vault," she said, holding the gold medal up while the ribbon hung from her neck. "But I doubt I'll be selected for Team USA."

"Well, you can be on my team any day."

"At least I kicked Alena Shenkova's butt in the vault," she said, and ran for the entrance behind Buck.

Jax and Ramsey exchanged pleasantries with Jack, and then began unloading their baggage with the help of a security guard. Jack helped Anna tie down the Hughes.

Out of ear shot from the others, Jack asked, "How's Buck?"

"In good spirits," she said. "*Vhy* you ask?"

"We have a sanction—big one."

Buck stood with Jules before the bullet proof glass wall of his favorite room—his fortress of solitude—or what his friends would affectionately refer to as his *Man Cave*. It served as his office and entertainment area, complete with an English style bar and pool table. A solarium with sunken pool extended out the rear, offering an unobstructed view of the ski area. The walls without windows or flat screen monitors were lined with bookcases holding a lifetime of memorabilia, and, surprisingly, even some books.

Anna and Charlotte, ever the modern business women, refused to degrade themselves to the boys' baseness. They simply called it, *The Library*.

While they were alone, Jules yanked on Bucks sleeve. "Grandpa, I'd like to get a few 'don't tell Mom moments' in while I'm here."

Buck smiled. He knew exactly what Jules wanted. Her mom frowned on Jules handling weapons of any kind. "No harm, no foul. No tell, no trouble. Rifles and guns are all set up down stairs. I gave Jack a heads up before we left." Buck winked at Jules, and ran his index finger and thumb across his lips to emphasize the point. "Keep your lips zipped and we'll be fine."

Anna ushered Jax and Ramsey into the *Library* and found Buck pouring a drink at the bar. "*Vould* anyone else care for something before we head to dinner?"

While Jules and her parents spent the next couple of days skiing—Buck, Jack, and Anna spent their time analyzing and preparing for Buck and Jack's sanction.

In the kneehole of the desk in the library, behind a brass logo label, were two buttons. One controlled specialized panels that lowered from the attic and covered the windows and doors. The result was a pure SCIF, or a Sensitive Compartmental Information Facility, virtually impregnable and unhackable.

Buck pressed the second button and a bookcase on the wall opened to reveal a staircase that lead to a thirty-two-by-sixty-four foot, soundproofed, environmentally controlled room. It housed the heart of his computer system BADDAY, his whole operations, actually. The length of the wall was lined with flat screen monitors, servers, communication equipment, and printers.

Buck inserted the disc with the sanction, and they went to work.

At night, when Jules and her parents weren't sightseeing and dining with Buck, or when her parents retired for the night in the residential wing, Jules stole as much time as she could in the soundproof gun range with Buck.

Sunday morning arrived faster than Jules wanted, but she couldn't wait to get to SPI. Grandpa Buck had said his goodbyes at Aspen-Pitkin County Airport—known as Sardy Field to the locals—Aspen's airport for the rich and famous. He had to head to DC on government business. Jules knew that wasn't one hundred percent true.

"So Grandpa, tell me something about your government business trip." Jules had a way of catching people off guard.

"I'm. . . "

The pause was a little, too long for Jules' taste. She moved close to Buck and whispered in his ear. "I know you're not really married to Char."

"What brought that up?" he said. "And anyway . . . you know I can't talk about my assignments."

"What if it's something illegal?" Jules asked.

Buck began rubbing his chin. *A tell*, thought Jules. *He's going to lie to me.*

"Honey, there's a fine line when it comes to terrorism between politically correct illegal and illegal," Buck said, drawing out the last illegal. "You have to understand the world we live in. Now is not the time for democrats, or liberals. I am not a republican either—I'm a patriot, and I make part of my living from that fact."

Buck kissed Jules on the top of her head. "I'll see you in a couple of weeks."

Jules watched as he turned and boarded the Corporation's Gulfsteam G550. She mused about what she knew to be fact.

Buck Axele Davidssen lived and breathed US Marine Corps his whole life. But, for twelve years—as an active Marine—he was trained and prepared for everything. It wasn't just about achieving his goals, but believing in himself. The Marine Corps motto said it all—Semper Fidelis—always faithful, always loyal to your comrades in arms, God, Country, and family.

On land, in the air, and on the sea—he performed as commanded, no questions asked. He defended the constitution and killed to protect America's freedom. The Corps was Buck's family, but something happened and Buck snapped. Three weeks shy of his twenty-ninth birthday, 9/11 occurred, and changed his views forever. Buck retired from the Corps as a captain.

Buck had another gift—computers and logic—he was a natural, and with his best friend Dr. Roy Singh, they created The Corporation, and amassed one of the best counter-terrorism tracking systems on the planet. Buck could count the people he trusted most on both hands. They were the Core members of his old unit who would take a bullet to protect his six (military jargon for rear end), and information technology specialists who would drop what they're doing in a heartbeat to work with him on a project.

The Corporation constantly grew with lucrative contracts from the DHS and the CIA. When Dr. Anna Semyonova joined the core group, talks began for building an Advanced Nanoscience Research Center. The Corporation funded the majority of the money to build the center. Additional funds began pouring in from the Alphabet Soup community, and two years later the South Padre Island Advanced Nanoscience Research Center in Texas was born.

Although the research center strove for the advancement of medical science through nanotechnology, teams of scientist explored alternate technologies to maintain America's leadership against the war on terrorism—foreign and domestic.

Buck and this group of freedom fighters worked under the protection of a Presidential Finding that allowed them to bypass the red tape of government bureaucracy. It was signed by his girlfriend, Charlotte "Char" Vice-Davidssen, the President of the United States of America.

4

SPI - South Padre Island, Texas
Sunday March 31st

Eight days after the National Championships, Jules feasted on the sites of South Padre Island as Anna circled the custom Hughes helicopter over her beach house—an architectural dream. The house sat on one of the larger islands of SPI on Laguna Madre Bay. The hundred area tract, owned by *The Corporation*, was just north of Edwin King Atwood Park, where civilization ended.

The SPI Nanoscience Laboratory complex and campus included the Nanoscience laboratory, the information technology center, and dorm style housing for staff and students. It sat directly across the lagoon on the main beach island. SPI Boulevard abruptly stopped a few

31

miles further north of the complex, even though the beach island continued another fifty plus miles.

Jules mingled with the guests at Anna's kick-off barbecue for the new students and staff. Only a handful of the twenty-four students who would start classes with Jules the next day were in attendance. Most of the guests were professors as well as colleagues—for lack of a better word—of Buck and Anna with whom Jules spent most of her time. Although she was not born with a silver spoon, everything always seemed to fall into place for her. This fueled her social awkwardness among peers her own age. She could count her closest friends on one hand, and they were mostly from her early childhood.

Jules comfort level radiated among intelligent and beautiful women, and while she attempted to mimic the grace and style of Anna, she never believed she could measure up to her beauty. What she didn't know was her peers saw her differently. To them, Jules was not only talented and extremely smart—she was exquisitely beautiful. However, her shyness and awkward social graces put forth an air of conceit, and this turned them off.

The funniest guy at the barbeque was Big John, a six-foot-four barrel of a man with a Popeye Doyle hat perched on his bald head. He wore a colorful bib with bold letters, which stated he was the "head chef". Jules had met Big John years earlier while vacationing in Miami with her mom. The big guy hadn't change a bit, except maybe his humor was funnier. He entertained the quests with his mastery of flipping skirt steaks over the dried mesquite in a rusted out fifty-five gallon drum that had to be as old as him. Dr. Roy Singh, a wiry six-footer and Grandpa Buck's longstanding friend, was goading Big John on.

Jules hesitated when the cute dark haired guy who had been following her around all day joined the conversation. Jules heard the term *socially inept* tossed around by family and members of the Corporation, she preferred to think of herself as just *ungraceful* around the opposite sex of her own age.

I can't figure out if he was gay or just plain shy like me. She had another thought, *Knowing Grandpa, the boy was probably assigned to guard me. Maybe I'll just mosey over like a Texan and find out.*

"Hey Jules," Big John said.

"Hey you, too," Jules said. "Got a good joke for me?" She flashed a smile toward Roy. "Hello, Dr. Singh."

Big John gave Jules a hug. "No, but I'll test that mind of yours. Do you know the secret to cooking Skirt steaks?"

Jules knew the answer, but played along, and put her index finger to her lips. "Hmmm . . . let me guess . . . the mesquite?"

"Nope," said Big John, "It's the rusted out barrel."

Jules, Roy, and shy boy laughed. "So guys . . . you going to introduce me to my new bodyguard?" Jules knew—from listening in on private conversations—that Big John was her main bodyguard, and she would take advantage of that fact.

33

Roy laughed and held out his hand toward Big John, who slapped a twenty in it. "Jules, please call me Roy." To Big John he said, "Told you." He turned toward Jules with shy boy in tow. "This young lad is my nephew Jai Singh who will be taking classes here as well . . . and shadowing you."

Jules looked up into Jai's deep brown eyes, took his extended hand and shook it. "Hello Jai, I'm Juliet Spenser, but call me Jules or get punched." A grin spread across her face. "Are you going to the Phish concert?"

Jai laughed. "Something tells me I am."

The exchange did not go unnoticed by Roy. He was well acquainted with Jules' tendencies to either under or over compensate regarding her emotional responses when dealing with young men. He wanted to say something to aid in her struggle but could only interject, "Jules, how are you faring with the other students?"

Jules smirked and then smiled. "Just fine and dandy."

"Have you seen the gym center?" Roy asked. "I understand that there is a separate gymnastics wing."

"I'll check it out when I get bored," she said, and took the large wrap that Big John had prepared for her. "See you later."

Jai looked on as Jules disappeared into the crowd of guests. Although it was the first time they had met, he somehow felt that he had known Jules for most of his life. His Uncle Roy was a close friend and associate of Jules' grandfather and had actually seen her often—through stories and pictures. Jai wasn't as gifted as Jules, but they had one thing in common: neither had ever dated. Jules was Jai's first love—maybe it was infatuation, but he was hoping to make whatever it was real.

A tear had formed in his right eye as he turned back toward his Uncle.

"Come on Jai," Roy said, as his nephew wiped his eye. "Let's go join the others at the Tiki bar, and have a beer."

"Thanks Uncle Roy, but . . . I think I'll just head back to the dorm."

"I hope you know what you're getting into," he whispered after his nephew's retreating form.

Jules was now hunting for her parents who were getting a tour of the beach house with Anna. Two of Jules' classmates blocked her path as she headed toward the front steps to Anna's deck. Jules started to steer to the left trying to avoid them, but they moved, blocking her path. Both of the girls were beautiful in Jules' opinion, amply stacked in all the right places and dressed in the latest fashion. Not to mention the expensive jewelry they were adorned with. Jules saw "rich-bitches" and expected a confrontation—with a dose of name calling.

Instead the beautiful girl with long blond hair extended her hand. "Hi, I'm Sandy . . . you're Jules, right? This is my friend Mary Francis."

"Yes, I'm Jules Spenser," she said while accepting a handshake from the stunning brunette, Mary Francis."

"Listen," said Sandy. "We're going to the Phish concert tonight and were hoping you'd like to join us."

"I was planning—" Jules paused as an extremely handsome six-foot tall blond boy joined the mix.

"Hi, I'm Gunther."

"I have to go," Jules said. She walked up the steps, and when she reached the deck, she turned back, looking down at the group. "Nice racks, girls. Don't miss the Hawaiian Tropic Bikini Contest," she whispered, and then she turned smartly on her heels and made her way toward the front door.

Jules found her mom and dad in Anna's home office.

Jax rose from her seat when Jules knocked on the open door. "Honey, we were just leaving. Dad and I are going back to the hotel to clean up and get our Phish gear on. Anna says you're staying here with her, and that you have an escort for the concert." She chuckled and then continued, "Look for us. The whole gang will be there tonight, and we'll be filming everything."

Jules gave her mom and dad a kiss, "See you later . . . love you." Jax waved goodbye as she and Ramsey left.

After they had left, Anna pressed a button on her desk and the door closed mechanically. "Jules, have a seat. Buck and I have a couple of presents for you, but instead of waiting, I think I'll give them to you now. But first things first: give me your right arm."

Anna injected a tracker in Jules' right shoulder.

"Ouch!"

"Suck it up Champ," Anna said. "Every core member gets one."

Then she handed Jules a funky looking device the size of a smartphone. "This is an R-CAT—developed by Roy and myself. It's the ultimate smartphone, camera, TV, and computer rolled into one. Only ten people in the world have one. You and Jai will be the eleventh and twelfth. The R-CAT has four channels, phone app one is your phone, phone app two is a party line to Buck, me, Roy, Jack, Emma, and Jai for a group calls. Apps three and four are not activated on your device."

Anna pointed to the color-coded buttons on top. "The R-CAT also has multiple functions: the Black button operates a taser function, and will be activated this week when you're trained in its use." Anna paused.

"What about the—"

Anna put up her hand and Jules stopped. "The Red, White, and Blue will be activated at a later date." Anna paused, her eyes said it all, and this time Jules didn't interrupt. "The R-CAT will send an alert to the group if it is more than twenty-two feet from you, and will also automatically shut down the device."

Twenty-two feet may sound odd to most people, but not to Jules—Twenty-two is a master number in numerology. "Is it waterproof?" Jules asked, smiling.

"Yes. So carry it with you at all times. There are hundreds of apps on this, so get familiarized with them. We have apps that the CIA and NSA don't have. Welcome to *The Corporation*."

Jules was stunned. "Wow! So tell me about the Red, White, and Blue buttons."

"When I think you're ready, they will be activated."

Jules let it go and started to rise.

"We're not done yet," Anna said. "Now for the fun stuff. Hit the first app button on the R-CAT."

The first app had a picture with a skull and bones. "Press it, Jules."

The next screen had logo images of Anna's beach house, a Ford truck, and a smiley face. Jules pressed the picture of Anna's house. There were buttons for the front, back, and garage doors. Next Jules pressed the Ford truck app. It had additional buttons for access and starting the truck, as well as a few other options.

Jules laughed. "What's the smiley button for?"

Anna laughed. "Buck says Texas girls drive trucks. I say Texas girls have more class. You decide. The smiley face operates my red Ferrari . . . use it whenever you wish."

Jules stood and hugged Anna. "Love you."

"The remote keys are hanging by the door," Anna said, and smiled. "That's if you prefer the old fashion way."

Jules was on a roll. "When is Buck coming?"

Anna wasn't sure and didn't want to lie. "He's dark right now, but I expect a call by Saturday."

Jules made a GMAB (Give Me a Break) face, but said nothing. She knew what *dark* meant. Grandpa was on a top secret mission.

"Okay, one more gift." Anna handed her a box.

Jules opened it, and stared at a Glock-26. It was called the *Baby Glock*, or ladies version—smaller, lighter, but just as powerful as the bigger version. She also saw the magazine in it. "Anna, I can't . . . mom would—"

"Buck says you've had plenty of practice and you're ready."

Jules picked up the gun, popped the magazine, ejected the round in the pipe, and then field stripped the Glock. She locked eyes with Anna while putting it back together again. "I know, but mom would lose it if she saw me with one." Jules said, and then snickered. "Come on, Anna— you know mom. She's not like Buck and you—she's the Dalai Lama, Gandhi, and the *Woodstock* writer Joni Mitchell all rolled into one."

"Fine," Anna said. "I'll hold onto it for now. Go mingle with the kids and have fun at the concert. But don't forget breakfast's at seven and class starts at eight a.m. sharp."

Jules started to leave when Anna had an afterthought. Wanting to see Jules' reaction, she shot out, "You have protection, right?"

"Anna!" Jules blurted. Jules smiled and left Anna shaking her head.

5

Isla Grand Beach Resort
Sunday Night March 31st

Dressed in her full Phish ensemble, which included a tie-dye T-shirt, worn-out shredded jeans, and bead necklace, Jules headed out of the house to the truck. She received hoots and hollers from the guys hanging out at the full service Tiki bar.

She saw Jai and waved for him to join her; he was going to follow her anyway. She might as well be in charge.

Fashionably late to the concert, Jules had no problem finding her mom and dad. Jax and the Phish Phreaks were up by the bandstand snapping off pictures and videos of the band and their group. Jules zeroed in on her mom's voice. Jax knew every song by heart.

Jax hugged her daughter. "I thought you'd never make it," she said, and handed Jules a backstage pass for the after party.

Jules declined. "Thanks mom, but I'm only staying for a little while."

True to her word, after the first set, Jules told Jai she was heading home—alone. Jai stood speechless as Jules disappeared through the crowd. On her way to the truck, she saw Mary Francis standing in the parking lot crying, and started toward her. But when Gunther appeared from nowhere, she changed her mind, and continued on to the truck. She was back at Anna's and in bed by ten p.m. She got to know her device by accessing each of the apps on her R-CAT, and was sound asleep by midnight—the device still in her hand.

Monday morning at six-thirty, Jules found Anna in the hearth room off the kitchen reading the local paper. A steaming cup of black coffee sat in arms reach of her. Every appliance and utensil shined, the kitchen was immaculate (just the way Anna liked life in general), and everything was perfect. A saucer with some kind of milk sat on a doily in the center of the table. The smell of fresh fried bacon was apparent, but there was a hint of vanilla in the air, too, but not French. It was coming from the coffee brewer.

Anna caught Jules inquiring sniffs. "It's a special Russian blend."

Jules poured herself a cup and sat next to Anna. "Vat kind?"

"Ha to you, too. How *vould* you like your eggs?" Anna asked, as she turned toward Jules, and stared her dead on.

"Scrambled *vith* bacon," Jules said, and leaped from the chair. "I'll make the toast."

Anna let the slurs go by. "Listen honey, I'd like you to try and make some friends today."

Jules' demeanor changed immediately. She hunched her shoulders and dipped her head. She basically just shut down, retreating into herself.

Just when Anna thought she had a handle on Jules' thought processes, and unique abilities, she would behave or think completely opposite in her expectations. Her character occasionally strayed outside the boundaries of known psychiatric diagnosis. At times she had proven to have a ruthless, almost sadistic streak, and appeared to be slightly psychopathic.

Jules lacked social skills, which was apparent when she strayed outside her comfort zone. For Jules, love and friendship were relative outside her inner circle of family, which included the inner core of The Corporation, and ultimately—not necessary to survival.

Anna had been working with Jules on her emotions for several years. She saw how her peers reacted to her aloofness, and even heard them call her a freak at times. Anna watched as Jules ate her breakfast with zero emotion. When she was finished she cleaned her plate, and left the house.

A tear formed and ran down Anna's cheek. Anna just wanted to reach out, pull her in, and hug and kiss her troubles away. But even the most perfect of roses have thorns, and she just got stung by Jules'. Anna sat sipping her coffee and worried that Jules would eventually push everything good away from her life.

Jules' attitude changed when she saw Dr. Singh and his nephew at the science complex. Instantly gone was her sourpuss face and robotic strut. Her frown had turned into a smile, and there was a hop and a skip to her pace. Jai and Roy were standing just outside the door to main auditorium where the orientation would be held. They appeared to be in deep conversation as Jules made her way down the hallway.

As she came into earshot, Roy stopped talking. He then turned abruptly and began walking her way. "See you in lab later," he said to Jules on his way past her. "And make sure he learns something, would you?" Roy nodded over his shoulder, indicating Jai.

Jules' frown returned when just she and Jai were left in the hallway.

"Morning, Jai," Jules said as she brushed by him into the auditorium.

"I'm thrilled to see you, too." Brokenhearted, all Jai could do was stare at her as she pranced down the aisle. He never expected anything to actually happen last night, but the way she just left him flat, hurt him deeply. He entered the auditorium and sat in the back row to sulk.

The first day of internship began with introductions, first by the professors, and then the students. Jules noted that Mary Francis Davenport and Gunther Baader giggled when Sandy Russell's name was called. Curiously, she was not present.

During lunch break, Jules, concerned about not seeing Sandy either at last night's concert, or today in class, accessed the I-SPY law enforcement database app on her R-CAT. She ran a search on Sandy Russell and her parents. The data showed that Sandy wasn't a child prodigy; she wasn't even a genius. Her parents were dirt rich, and major donors to the program. They had obviously pulled some strings to get Sandy enrolled.

Throughout the rest of the day, which couldn't end fast enough for Jules, she continually thwarted away advances from Gunther and some of the other boys. She declined an offer from her parents to attend the second Phish concert, and instead, spent the evening researching her other classmates.

As she stored the information of each student away in the private database between her ears, she dwelled on Sandy.

As she stored the information of each student away in the private database between her ears, she dwelled on Sandy.

Tuesday morning, Jules was out the door by seven a.m. hoping to catch a perfect sunrise. It was not to happen. She was the first student in the lecture lab, and used the free time to continue her investigations.

Across the bridge in the staff housing units, Dr. Bryce Kellogg leaned against the railing of her balcony and stared out at the cloudy marine layer that ruined a perfectly good sunrise. Unlike the perfect sunsets on Laguna Madre Bay, sunrise was the same every day since she had moved to the island—cloudy. The locals had many theories to the phenomenon, but Bryce knew that it was caused by the warm air currents well above the shore meeting the cooler water that circled in from the gulf. A temperature inversion occurred that created a layer of haze as the cold air pushed under the warmer air. Bryce also knew that by the time she got to her office at seven-thirty, the brume layer would've burnt off, and it would be another perfect day on South Padre Island.

Dr. Kellogg adjusted her thick granny glasses as she walked from her office into the adjoining lab room. With her over-sized, rainbow maxi dress, and her light brown hair twisted into a bun, Bryce appeared more like a hippie on her way to a Phish concert than an advanced nanostructure scientist.

Her smile was not so much happy looking, as it came off more like a smirk. This went unnoticed by Jules who was buried in her laptop, her fingers moving a mile a minute. Dr. Kellogg was not surprised Jules was the first student in attendance for her lecture on advanced biopolymer-based nanostructures.

"Good morning, Jules."

Jules raised her eyes for a brief moment. She liked Dr. Kellogg and her nerdy, hippy look. "Morning, Dr. Kellogg."

"It's Bryce, Jules."

Jules nodded. "Sorry, Bryce . . . love the outfit," she said, and then resumed her typing. She would have to hurry, for the lecture would start in fifteen minutes, and the other students would be showing up shortly. Jules' eyes twinkled. She was on to something.

Orientation continued until four p.m. with Anna giving her wrap up speech in the auditorium. Jules had visited every lab, and met every professor and department head in the facility. The campus also had a full service exercise gym, and a separate wing with world class gymnastic equipment. Jules was sure her grandfather had a role in that. Later that evening, she had dinner with her parents at Isla Grand Beach Resort, and again stayed for Phish's first set before catching a ride back to the complex with Jai. He was beginning to grow on her, but she still wouldn't let him in to her *Quan*—her inner sole.

Jai leaned toward her in order to kiss her cheek, but Jules was already out of the golf cart before he got half way there. She bid him goodnight at the bridge. There was no argument from him. He was left speechless.

Jules found herself alone in the house and spent the rest of the night on Anna's deck.

They're all out, probably having fun, thought Jules. *Not me, though. I have to find out what happened to Sandy.* Jules was in la la land by midnight.

At school, Wednesday morning, there was still no answer when Sandy's name was called. Mary Francis blurted just loud enough for the people in her vicinity to hear. "Bet she's in Paris with some gigolo."

Jules gave Mary Francis *the stare.*

Mary Francis stared right back at her and innocently asked, "What?"

Jules looked away. She immediately came to the conclusion that she didn't like Mary Francis.

The rest of the day went as expected, but later that evening, during dinner, Jules brought up the subject of the missing Sandy, but Anna quickly dismissed it.

Fine, thought Jules. *Tomorrow I'm interning with Dr. Roy Singh, and we'll see just what else BADDAY the talking computer can do. Anna and Sandy's parents probably think Sandy blew off classes to go jet setting. That's how rich girls roll, right? I think not in this case. You don't get selected for a program like this and just blow it off. Something happened to Sandy, and I will find out why on my own.*

Wednesday was also the last day of the final Phish concert. Once again, Jules' mom, Jax's whole gang of Phish Phreaks descended on SPI. The group was now over thirty strong and many of them, like Jax, followed Phish religiously around the country to every event. Jax's group was staying at the Isla Grand Beach Resort by the beach where Phish was performing.

Jules stayed home instead, and after dinner, she helped Anna clean up.

"If you need to blow off some steam," Anna said. "There's always the gymnasium."

"Nah, not tonight. If you need me I'll be outside enjoying the view and catching up with e-mails."

Anna started for her office but turned back to Jules, a look of concern on her face. "Honey if you need to talk, you know where to find me."

"I'm good, I'm just worried about Sandy."

Jules strolled outside and began flipping through her messages. Her Mom had taken tons of pictures and videos, and e-mailed them. She watched the sunset, and Big John was right: it was much better than Key West.

A half hour later, when the island began to glow with lights and the festivities had started in full swing, Jules called it a night. She knocked on the opened door to Anna's office.

Anna immediately noticed the concerned look on Jules' face. "Honey, vat's the matter?"

Jules walked in, and without joking about Anna's accent, Jules sat down and replied with all seriousness, "Anna . . . I think I'll take that Glock-26 now."

6

Ocean Boulevard
Thursday April 4th

Jules was out the door at five on the nose with her go bag—a collection of goodies prepared by her grandpa for survival. Curfew was midnight to five a.m. and she knew Anna would check her R-CAT to see what time she left the house. Everything in Anna's house was programmed. Jules assessed the two vehicles parked side by side and smiled. She hit the first two buttons on the second row of the remote. The Ferrari roared to life, *time to clear the mechanisms and let the big dog eat.*

Jules drove over the bridge that connected Anna's island with the complex. The guard at the booth waved her through—her picture and ID appeared on his monitor. The guard knew exactly who the precious cargo was seated behind the steering wheel of the Ferrari. The same process occurred as she pulled to the booth leaving the complex. Jules made the left onto Ocean Boulevard and ran the gears.

World class gymnast aside, Jules' d*evil-may-care* attitude was never more apparent then when she got behind the wheel to test her skills and push the envelope.

The Ferrari onboard computer system was programmed to announce vocalized speed changes at intervals of fifty kilometers per hour, and a sexy female voice chirped, "Speed two-hundred-fifty kilometers per hour."

It was also programmed to activate on Jules's voice command. It was a Ferrari after all, and it was loaded.

Jules smiled, punched her fist in the air, and calculated her speed. "One-fifty-four point three-four, miles per hour, not bad. Show me what you got."

Mother Nature had formed the perfect barrier of dunes. It was his own castle made of sand and seaweed on a small peninsular—a stone's throw south from Island Adventure Park. It was his favorite place for sex, and leering at the woman at the park, or in passing cars. Tony was a perv, plain and simple.

Exhausted and feeling no pain from the drugs he had taken, he had nodded off shortly upon returning to his hideout alone after last call at a local bar.

Awakened by the loud roar, Tony popped up his head from the dune just in time to see the red Ferrari fly by. That aroused his interest.

A Ferrari on SPI was like a rack on a bull—not happening, he thought.

The Ferrari was long gone by the time he got his act together. He got on his motorcycle, and rode the shore line north.

Where was the Ferrari going to go anyway, he thought. *The road ended in a mile.*

When she blew past the sign warning: *Road ends in 1 mile,* she pressed harder. Traveling at over two hundred-seventy feet per second Jules quickly calculated that she'd need about twenty-two-hundred feet to stop.

"Come on already . . . say it"

Five-hundred feet later, the computerized voice said, "Speed three-hundred kilometers per hour."

Jules blinked. "One-eighty-six point four-one, better, but I know you got more."

With sunrise almost two hours away, and the road narrowing from the accumulation of windblown sand on both sides—Jules made the call. She released the gas pedal and gently tapped the breaks. Five taps later she reduced her speed to 200 kph. Another two taps and the Ferrari announce her speed of 150 kph, or 93 mph. Jules slammed the brake pedal to the floor. The Ferrari fishtailed slightly side to side when she compensated with the steering wheel from loss of traction with the accumulated sand on the road.

Close call—

Jules had thirty plus feet of real estate left when the Ferrari finally came to a stop, and she shut the beast down.

The island narrowed at this point to less than one-hundred yards. Jules stared out at the lapping gulf that danced before her. Hypnotized by the rhythm of each breaking wave she removed her shorts. Clad in a one-piece suit, she grabbed her Go Bag, and let the breathing sea draw her in. Time for a swim.

Running across the sand, she thought about how she got where she was now, and more importantly, when she decided her career path.

It all started three years ago:

Jules loved gymnastics, physics, and information technology; she also wanted to help mankind. She got that from her mom and dad. They were down to earth parents who only wanted the best for Jules. They didn't smoke, drink, or do drugs. Their only vice was following Phish around the country, they never missed an event.

When Nanoscience became the hot subject, Jules thought she could combine both disciplines into a rewarding career, and help mankind at the same time. A child prodigy, she had been taking college level classes since she was eleven. She graduated high school at thirteen.

She fell in love with gymnastics at age six, and was a natural. She even managed to squeeze in fifteen to twenty hours of practice a week on her tight schedule, and she excelled. Jules belonged to a local gymnastics club that was sponsored by her grandpa's company. She never had a problem finding a gym to practice at. Her trust fund, started by her grandpa was one she couldn't personally touch until she was twenty-one, but took care of everything else.

Her private coach was an ex-Olympic champion and just happened to work for The Corporation. This did not make her popular among most of the other gymnasts, who gave eight to ten hours a day to the sport. Jules didn't care, she had her own goals, and nothing would stop her.

Her dad was a communications engineer, and contracted his services to several major sports networks. He had seniority in a tight union, and pulled strings to work at all her major competitions. Her mom volunteered her services to ensure that Jules got whatever she needed.

Grandpa Buck did what he could, but was always travelling. Her mom said that he had an important job with the government, which was why he couldn't always make special occasions. Jules went along with her excuse, even though she believed there was more to it. Most of her Grandpa's other friends and colleagues, as he put it, were Marines, except for Dr. Roy Singh who was the only one with a degree. In fact, he had three PhDs. Jules would catch up with him, too.

Grandpa Buck gave her access to his business computer network and always made sure she had the latest equipment. When she approached Grandpa Buck with her goals and future plans, he said he had just the right people to help her. At the time, his girlfriend was a powerful lawyer and political figure in Washington DC. Not only that, Dr. Charlotte Vice was an old money billionaire. She pulled strings to get Jules enrolled in Johns Hopkins accelerated physics and information technology programs. When Dr. Anna Semyonova joined the tight group, she ensured that Jules excelled.

Jules didn't break for the summer; her goal was to walk away with double master degrees in three years. None of this was a mystery to anyone who knew her.

Her mom and dad had wanted to surprise her for her fifteenth birthday and had pulled out all the stops to get family and friends together at their home in New Jersey for the occasion. Buck had borrowed Char's Learjet 85 to pick up Jules, and fly her home for the weekend. Char couldn't make the trip, but sent along a fat check to buy whatever she wanted.

Jules had flown in the Lear a few times and was flicking through channels on the big dropdown flat screen TV. Grandpa Buck was sipping a scotch and staring at a GPS overlay on his laptop. Jules gave him a poke in the side. "Hey, Grandpa, know what?" Jules giggled. "I think I'm smarter than you now."

Buck laughed. "I think so too, honey. So I guess that means you're all growed up."

"You're funny, Grandpa. It's grown up . . . not growed up."

"Well then, grown up, you can call me Buck from now on."

Jules giggled again. "Okay, Buck." Then she full out cackled. "Nah. . . Grandpa is fine with me. . . Buck." She fell out of the seat laughing her butt off.

Buck bent over to pull her up. "You might be a genius honey, but you're still a little girl at heart."

She shook the memories from her mind, and with her R-CAT secured to her left wrist, and her survival knife—a gift from grandpa—strapped to her right thigh, she stepped into the water. Expecting an icy impact she tensed. Only to relax and embrace the warm drops of sea that lashed out, and basked her face in a coat of delicate salt spume.

Jules swam straight out until she hit a sand bar several hundred feet from shore. The depth of the crystal clear water never dropped deeper than five feet. The moon cast just enough light that she could clearly see a school of fish swim by. She laid out on the sand, her thoughts turned to the first couple of days on SPI, and the disappearance of

Sandy Russell. Jules could read Anna like a book, too. She knew Anna was just as protective of her as Mom, and was covering something up.

You might be a spoiled brat, Sandy, but you still don't deserve what may have happened to you.

As she started to head back to shore, a pole with a boating flag floated by. Jules retrieved it. The flag was the symbol for F, a red diamond on a white field. She pulled out her knife; extracted the magic marker from the water proof handle, and wrote 'Jules Island' on the flag. She secured it in the middle of her private island and swam back to shore.

Yeah it was worth it, she thought when she looked at the Ferrari. *I'm going to miss the competitions, but I'm not going to miss the training.*

She took the winter off from school to train full time for the National Championships. Twelve hour days at the gym killed her, but some of the other girls finally warmed up to her—none among the elite gymnasts. The Team USA coach saw something in her, and sent her an invitation to the qualifiers. Jules placed in the top twenty-four, which gave her a shot to make Team USA.

Jules hopped into the Ferrari without opening the door. She pressed the ignition button and said, "Ignition on." The Ferrari fired up. "I'm the National Champion of Vaulting," Jules yelled at the top of her lungs. She took in the view on the way back to Anna's house.

A motorcycle power slid to a stop as Jules, and the Ferrari blew by it. She smiled. *Another adventure seeker perhaps, pursuing the thrill of speed in the early morning.*

It was a little after six and Anna was probably up already looking for her. Jules glanced at her right shoulder where the tracker was injected, and laughed. *Anna knows exactly where I am.*

Tony caught up to the Ferrari as it pulled up to the guard booth to the Nanoscience Research campus. He would find out later who the mystery blonde driver was.

7

Anna's Island
Thursday April 4th

Anna was sitting on the front deck with a hot mug of something, and reading a folder of papers. Jules could see the steam rising from the top of the cup as she drew closer.

A snow leopard appeared from the corner of the house, and stopped Jules in her tracks. Its gait was more of a shy crawl then a stalk, and it sat down next to Jules.

"Is this real?" Jules blurted.

Anna's eyes beamed toward Jules. "It's Emma's first robot." After a pause Anna calmly asked Jules, "So how did she handle?"

Jules was waiting for more, but none came. Emma was Dr. Emma Dash, Anna's cousin, and would be Jules instructor for today's classes. Jules had never met Emma, but heard all the stories. Anna was incredibly beautiful, but word on the street from grandpa's crew was that Emma was hotter.

"She's hot and beautiful, just like you," Jules said. "I needed to shake some things out, and took her out for a run."

"How fast?"

"Three-hundred when I blew past the sign." Jules knew that Anna thought in metrics. She ran her hands through the leopard's faux fur. "Damn, it's life-like."

Anna smiled. "You have to start further south. Andy Bowie Park works. I got her to three-fifty, and she still had more."

Jules smiled back at her after calculating that three-fifty kilometers was two-hundred-seventeen MPH and change. "Do we have time for another run?"

"No, go get ready. I'll make you a nice breakfast . . . and make a lot of noise. Emma would sleep until noon if I let her."

As she climbed the stairs of the deck, Anna stood, and the leopard leaped onto the deck next to her. Jules stopped and stared. Anna was a few years older than her mom, but she had that rare beauty that was hard to look away from. Anna's code name was the Panther. At five foot ten, and athletically built, it was her gait that earned her the moniker. Anna's eyes were a rare shade of blue, a piercing cobalt hue that sparkled. With her platinum hair in a ponytail, her slender stalk of neck drew the onlooker to her other assets.

Her body contouring, off white, soft leather jacket and pantsuit enhanced every curve of her body. With the zipper of the jacket halfway down, her breasts stretched the red, low cut cami she wore underneath, causing Jules' eyes to linger. The stare was not sexual, but an acknowledgement of her perfection. In Jules' mind Anna was a Goddess.

"Are you coming or not?" Anna asked.

Knocked from her trance, Jules blurted, "Sorry, but you make me feel flat-chested."

"Jules, I know you better than you think. I called Sandy's parents, and they did not seem concerned. They apologized and said, 'It's Sandy being Sandy.' Jules, she's a spoiled brat, and the local police have evaluated the matter, and they agree—"

"But—"

"But nothing, honey—it's out of our hands. Now go get ready . . . by the way, you're far from flat-chested." Anna said, and smiled at Jules as she passed. "I laid out some new clothes for you."

Jules ran by Anna and up the stairs. On her queen size bed, was an assortment of T-shirts, shorts, Vika and Quicksilver leather jackets and pantsuits. Jules jumped in the shower and brushed her teeth while the hot water exhilarated her. She toweled off and wrapped her hair in a ponytail. Her baby blue eyes stared back at her from the mirror. She admired her naked body. *Hah, I'm hot, too, Anna.*

She flipped through the T-shirts that Anna had piled up, and chose the camouflage US Marine Snake Eater T. She threw it on sans bra. Next she rummaged through the shorts and chose the colorful Quicksilver cycling shorts. She gazed toward her nightstand at the Glock-26, and laughed. "Nah."

Every time she visited with Grandpa Buck there was one of those *'don't tell mom'* moments. Grandpa would sneak her down to his shooting range in the basement of Angel's Landing. Over the years she became a sharpshooter. The hand guns were heavy, but grandpa finally found the perfect gun for her hand. The Glock-26 was the perfect protection for the young woman on the go.

Jules grabbed her backpack with all the other goodies in it, and then started for her bedroom door—she stopped and went back to the nightstand. She picked up the Glock, and smiled—*maybe I'll check out the gun range after school.* She tucked the Glock in her bag and left the room. As Jules passed the next room, she heard the shower. *Emma must be up.* She jogged down the stairs to find Anna frying up eggs and bacon.

Anna turned toward Jules. "There's fresh coffee—help yourself. Do you *vant* your eggs on a plate or in a wrap?"

"Wrap!"

Jules was on her second cup of coffee when Emma shuffled into the kitchen. Her platinum hair was styled in a chic pixie. She wore a white silk stretch body cami and candy-apple red Vika leather pants. Pink bunny slippers completed her attire. Emma went straight to the coffee pot.

"How *vas* the flight?" Anna inquired.

Emma smiled mischievously and blinked, her long lashes flitted over her emerald eyes. With the dark blue rims and flecks of gold around the pupil, they dazzled like golden fireworks. "Me bum is killing me, but D.C. was fun. So . . . what does the new world champion of gymnastics think of South Padre Island?"

Jules peered into Emma eyes, but not for long. *OMG! Emma is built like a brick shithouse and what a British accent.* "I'm the National Champion, Emma . . . but talking about World Class . . . nice rack," Jules said and snickered.

Anna and Emma laughed, too. "You've been hanging around Buck too much," Emma said.

Emma eyed Jules over her mug of coffee. "So honey we're about the same size. Feel free to go through my wardrobe.

Jules giggled, tapping her chest. "Yeah, right, then I'll really look flat-chested."

Anna turned toward the clock when it dinged and saw it was seven-thirty. "Jules, there's a few golf carts in the garage. Why don't you take one and head over to the complex?"

Jules got the hint and left. *Bet they're going to talk about grandpa.* At the front door Jules paused. "Anna, I heard the guys talking about a gun range."

That brought a smile to Anna's beautiful face. "It's in the lower level and you're programmed for access."

Jules looked toward her shoulder where the tracker was injected.

Anna's smile grew wider. Emma chuckled causing most of the coffee in her mouth to spill on her ample chest. "Damn—now I have to change," Emma said.

"No, Jules," Anna said. "BADDAY controls access though biometrics. Emma and I are going tonight before the demo if you'd like to join us."

"Deal," Jules said, as she pushed through the front door.

Jules drove the golf cart into the designated cart area where maintenance staff would give it a once over with a damp towel and charge the battery. The cart would be parked in a corresponding slot number.

Jules passed through security. The Glock in her backpack appeared on the screen, but an alert appeared on the guard's monitor that explained she was approved for carry. She found the corridor that led to the lower level, and placed her hand on the touch screen next to the bulletproof glass doors. A message appeared on the screen that read—Jules Spenser - Access granted.

The glass door opened.

The first door on the right was labeled 'Gun Range', but Jules continued down the hall reading the labels on the other doors. She stopped when she saw flight simulators, and entered.

A man who appeared to be her grandpa's age wearing Marine Corps BDU (Battle Dress Uniform) camouflage pants and cap, and a black Tee with USMC across the back—was working on a simulator with a sign that stated—CH-53E Super Stallion. He turned as Jules approached the simulator.

"Hey Jules," he said.

"Gunny?"

"Ah, you remembered," Master Gunnery Sergeant USMC (retired)—Bob 'Gunny' Denis said. "What brings you down here?"

"Just looking," she said. "What else do you have down here?"

"Follow me. I got something to show you."

The fifth simulator had a sign that read—Hughes MD-530F. "This is the flight simulator that Anna learned to fly on at NASA. It belonged to the CIA, and Anna got it for free as part of her deal."

"What deal?" Jules asked, rather surprised. She was never fully informed of the details involved in Anna's defection to the US.

"She promised to play nice with the CIA, but only if she could become part of The Corporation."

"Gunny what do I have to do to get some time in that?"

"It's pretty wide open. There are five people including Emma."

"Emma? I just don't picture her flying a helicopter."

"Jules, you'd be surprised what Emma can do." Gunny said. "Hell, I didn't think she'd pass the sniper test either. But I'll tell you what: I'll bet you get your license before her."

"Sign me up Gunny." Jules looked at her watch—it was twenty to eight. "I have to get to class. See you later."

Gunny watched as Jules left the simulator room. *A chip off old Buck's shoulder*, he thought. Gunny served in Nam with Buck's older brother Jameson—he was KIA (Killed in Action) three weeks after Gunny shipped back to the states.

Jules thought about stopping in the gun range to squeeze off a few rounds before class, but thought better about it. *I can't be late on the first day, and it will be fun to shoot with Anna and Emma. And besides—I'd sure like to see how Emma pulls off a double handed shot with those two big balloons in the way.*

8

SPI School for Advance Nanoscience Research
Thursday April 4th

From the front of the classroom, Jules took in the view of the sixteen lab stations. Two of the stations in the back row had reserved signs on them for visiting professors and staff. The others had cards with the students' names written on them. Jules laughed when she saw that shy Jai Singh was her lab mate

At the first break, she would process everyone in the class through her R-CAT and store the results. Among other reasons, she was curious as to how the other teams were chosen.

At ten to eight Emma walked into the lab classroom in cowboy boots, she was all business. She walked to one of the whiteboards and printed her name, Dr. Emma

Dash in perfect letters. Then she printed the class name, Advanced Nanofabrication, Characterization, and Bionanotechnology.

Jules took a quick look around the room and noticed everyone was staring at Emma. Most of the guys were drooling, including Jai. *Okay, maybe he's not gay.* Gunther "the hottie" Baader was definitely drooling. She also noted another girl was missing—his lab partner, Mary Francis Davenport.

Jai leaned over toward Jules. "Dr. Dash is hot."

Not gay, just shy, and only with me it seems. Jules gave him an elbow in the side.

"You don't get it—do you?" Jai said. *Damn, everybody in the class knows that I like Jules, but her. She's never had a boyfriend before—doesn't even know the signs. The only way she is going to know is if I come right out and say it.*

Emma walked to the front of the class with all eyes on her. "I am Dr. Dash and I'll be your instructor for the next two weeks. Our program is tried and true—it works. There are six professors and we rotate every two weeks. When I'm not teaching, I will be in the nanotechnology lab, or the nanobiotechnology lab doing my own research and working with interns. While I'm on campus I will be available for private discussions."

Hands went up, Emma schussed them. And the hands went down.

Jules looked toward Gunther. Keep it in your pants—perv.

Emma continued. "In the next two weeks we will discuss nanofabrication and characterization of semiconductor devices, including the Semiconductor Roadmap and implications. We will explore the interactions between biological systems and nanostructure surfaces. Studies will include the characterization of selected biopolymer-based nanostructures and their application in materials and structure fabrication. We will push the fringes of physical theory, supercomputing resources, and visualization of quantum modeling. Concepts will include the enhancement of nanodevices, nanoparticles, and nanoscale phenomena that occurs within the discipline of nanotechnology.

"In the laboratory, you will work on a range of equipment, such as plasma etches, chemical vapor deposition, metallization, wet chemical stations, thermal, lithography, X-ray Photoelectron Spectroscopes, and the Nuclear Magnetic Resonance machines. Upon completion of our program, you will have the tools to imagine and create systems that can be used for advancements in nanobiological and nanotechnical research."

Emma walked around the classroom. "Any questions before I begin?"

Hands shot up.

She pointed at the hot looking guy. "Yes, Gunther."

"Dr. Dash, will we be working on the cyclotron?" he asked.

"Not in this class," Emma said, "But later in the program a select few will."

71

All the other hands went down. Jules smirked. *Emma's already flirting.*

Emma dimmed the lights and began.

🔫

Jules was familiar with the lecture content and most of the equipment. Ten more minutes and it was lunch break. She was interning in the IT data center with Dr. Singh the rest of the day, and couldn't get there fast enough.

At the lunch break, she had to ditch Jai and ducked into the women's room. Jules ran a few of her classmates through the I-SPY app. *Good one, Roy and Anna.* The app combined the law enforcement databases of the CIA, NSA, FBI, and NIBRS, the National Incident-Based Reporting System. The database included criminal history records, law enforcement incident reports, records of judicial actions and decisions, and watch lists of known and suspected terrorists.

Jules had expected to be the youngest in the class—not even close. There were two girls and a guy who were younger. Most of the kids in the class were in their mid to late twenties, shy Jai Singh was twenty-one. Peter Lin's real first name was Yongzhouxiang.

OMG, how did they get Peter out of that? I'll have to spend some time with this one. And then there was twenty year old German hottie, Gunther Baader. Jules felt a hot flash run through her body. Hmmm maybe it's time for a little experimentation. Yo, Anna, about that protection?

Today's missing girl was Mary Frances "Miffy" Davenport, *another rich bitch.* Jules was laughing when she walked out of the women's room.

Shy Jai was waiting. "What's so funning?"

"Miffy is missing."

"Who's Miffy?"

🔫

Dr. Singh caught up with Jules and Jai as they were walking into the cafeteria. "Big John is barbequing again at Anna's. Do you want to go out or eat in?"

"Is Emma going?" Jules asked, in a snooty manner.

Jai laughed. "Jules is jealous. Dr. Dash is so hot."

Roy laughed, too. "Soooo . . . you met *Vixen.*"

"Who?"

"Vixen is Emma's handle," said Roy.

"Figures," Jules said. "Yeah, let's go, Big John is so funny."

"Jules, do you have a handle?" Jai asked.

What she wanted to say was, my handle is 'Schizoid'. I'm a socially inept daredevil and paranoid around members of the opposite sex who are not family—just ask Dr. Semyonova.

Instead she snickered. *For some reason I'm warming up to Jai.* "My friends call me 'Parker', you know the girl from the show *Leverage.* They say I'm an emotionally impulsive daredevil. I'm also socially inept, and have great physical self-control. I'm an acrobat, a genius, and a kickass—just like *Parker*." Jules gave Jai a pop in the arm. "I'm twenty pounds of crazy in a five pound bag."

"Parker it is," Jai said. "But I think you look more like the girl *Clarke* from *The 100*."

"Come on, let's go," Jules said, and smiled. *Yeah Clarke is hot*, she thought. "My golf cart is right outside the door."

Roy watched as the two prodigies scooted ahead of him. "Good luck, Jai. Anna has her work cut out with that *Wildcard*," he said in a low voice to no one in particular.

When Jules floored the cart over the bridge to Anna's island, Jai and Roy held on for dear life. Seated at the Tiki bar were two men whom she hadn't seen in a long time. They appeared to be in deep conversation with Anna, Big John, and a man she had never met.

They stopped talking when the golf cart pulled up and turned toward speed racer Jules. The shorter guy with a well-manicured Van Dyke beard was Micky Livingston, Director of Homeland Security Investigations. The silver haired man, who was almost as big as Big John was DCI Snowdan Jones, Director of the CIA. Both men were in suits and it was eighty-six degrees. Jules had met them both several years back, and knew that Grandpa worked with both of them.

Something happened to Grandpa Buck was Jules's first thought. Her second thought—*this has something to do with Sandy and Miffy. Clear the mechanism, and stay cool.*

Jules got a big hug from both men.

Mr. Livingston and Mr. Jones can read me like a book.

Micky spoke first. "Grandpa is fine honey. How are Dr. Semyonova and Dr. Singh treating you?"

Jules smiled. "I love it here. Anna and Roy are the best, and they're both keeping me busy."

"Good then," Micky said. "Dr. Semyonova, Dr. Singh, and Dr. Dash will be demonstrating some of their new robotics tonight. Then I'm taking the group to dinner. You and Jai are welcome to join us."

Damn, Jules thought. *Micky is always so professional, but I have other plans.* "Sorry, I was going to spend some time with mom tonight."

Anna beat her to the punch. "Your Mom and Dad will be joining us, honey."

Rats, thought Jules. "Fine then," she said. "Hey, Big John how about one of those wraps?"

"Hey, Jules," Big John said. "Have you met Greg?"

Jules assessed the six foot slightly graying man with a trimmed beard and a colorful Hawaiian shirt that appeared to be pressed just like his shorts.

Greg offered his hand to Jules. "Hello Jules, I'm Greg Correa and you're Buck's granddaughter right?"

Jules smiled. *Aha the ex-CIA guy.* "Yup, that's me, Jules Spenser at your service."

Big John handed Jules a skirt steak wrap. She excused herself and ran up to her bedroom—minus Jai. She had some searches to run.

Forty minutes later she returned to see Roy and Jai on the golf cart. She let Roy drive, and then followed him through the data center, where he was in his environment and a total chatterbox. Pointing at equipment and talking to everyone, all the way to his twenty-four foot square corner office. Jules entered first and skipped to the window for a look. From the second floor she could see the Laguna Madre Bay on the other side of Anna's island; she could also see Anna and her guests at the Tiki bar.

As she turned toward Roy's desk she caught another structure at the far end of Anna's island. *I wonder why no one mentioned that. I'll just have to mosey on down and take a peek for myself. Look at me thinking Texan.*

Roy's desk was surrounded by five thirty-two inch touch screen monitors. On the one wall not lined with bookcases were two seventy inch monitors. All the screens were in hibernation mode. Roy sat at his desk, while Jules and Jai pulled up two chairs besides him.

Roy looked up at the box on the ceiling with a three-hundred-sixty degree eye. "BADDAY . . . say hello to

76

Jules." Roy didn't have to look up, that was for show. Smaller sensors were installed throughout the complex and on Anna's island. The sensor scanned anyone who passed, and with a three-hundred-sixty degree eye, BADDAY didn't miss anything. The computer knew who Roy was by biometric scanning as soon as he walked in the room. The system knew who Jules and Jai were, too. BADDAY was also programmed to accept voice commands from Roy, Anna, Buck, and Jack Mameli. Jack was Buck's Marine buddy and right hand man.

"Hello, Jules," BADDAY said, with an obvious Russian accent, and then began rattling off her life history.

"Dr. Singh, what is BADDAY, and can it—" Jules paused. "She sounds a lot like Anna. Can she scan photo and video against a database and find similar occurrences."

Roy laughed and began his spiel. "First thing Anna did when she got access to BADDAY was tinker with the voice. Think of BADDAY as the ultimate security system. It's a global anti-terror tracking system that constantly searches the internet and communication frequencies for acts of terrorism against America. It can acquire anything with a CPU. BADDAY has the ultimate in encryption systems. Your Grandfather is constantly making enhancements to the algorithms. Our thermal GPS/ISP imagining, facial recognition, and biometric scanning is par none. Anna has pushed the boundaries of science with her environmental quantum modeling node on the CBRNE (Chemical, Biological, Radiological, Nuclear, and high-yield Explosives) detection system. Not to mention nanotechnology configurations."

Roy opened his drawer and took out a tracking injector. "With Anna's programmable nanobots, every member of The Corporation is tracked. Also anyone injected by us that we want to monitor. BADDAY is also the security system for the complex, Angel's Landing, our strategic warehouses, and even President Char Vice-Davidssen's law offices and suites in DC. BADDAY has access to most of the government law enforcement databases. Over the years we have added enhancements to their systems and created apps they don't have.

"BADDAY found that meta-material on K2 several years ago that became the core material used on the new cyclotron. There are four clones of BADDAY at alternate secure sites—one is Angel's Landing. BADDAY is standalone and does not interface with our super computers used for research or the business systems. For security and government compliance the super computers and business system are constantly updated at two other secure sites."

"Wow, Grandpa Buck never described it like that."

"What are you looking to do, Jules?" Roy asked.

"Two girls are missing from school. My mom has lots of pictures and video from the last few days. I'm hoping they appear in one of the photos or video with the person who might have taken them."

"Anna said you might be asking about that." Roy said. "I have BADDAY searching now against all video feeds on the island. The problem is that there's not much to work with. Most of the smaller hotels and shops shut down before and after spring break. So they don't invest in security systems."

Jules frowned. "Well, it's worth a shot if BADDAY can do it."

"Bring me what you have, and we'll give it a shot."

"Thanks, Dr. Singh." Jules said and smiled. *Bet you're going to tell me BADDAY couldn't find anything.*

"How about we go through the apps, and I'll show you what BADDAY can do."

"Sounds great. Where's Buck?"

Dr. Singh appeared caught off guard. Jules watched as he pushed a button on the desk, and BADDAY stopped talking.

Huh, bet he turned off the voice activation just in case. I bet BADDAY, Roy, and Anna knew exactly where Buck and Jack are. From the look on Roy's face, Jules knew Grandpa Buck was safe.

Roy coughed into his hand. "Don't know Jules, but I expect to hear from him soon."

Jules let it go, and they spent the rest of the afternoon going through apps and capabilities of BADDAY. At four-thirty, Roy excused Jules and Jai for the day.

"Thank you Roy. I think I'll go back to Anna's and take a power nap." She gave Jai the eye. "I'll see you tonight then."

Jai stood by Roy's desk as Jules left.

Good. He got the hint. With my access to BADDAY, I can write my own queries against mom's videos. If Anna and Roy don't bring up the missing girls, I won't either.

9

Anna's Island
Thursday April 4th

Jules left Jai at the lab with Dr. Roy Singh. He didn't even attempt to follow her. *It's time for some serious snooping around Anna's island.* Nobody was around when Jules pulled up to the house. She slipped into a one-piece bathing suit and shorts, and took her golf cart south down a paved path. On her R-CAT she selected the thermal GPS app and zoomed in on Anna's island. The island was somewhat kidney shaped, but thinned to fifty feet at the center. The northern section was roughly a seven hundred by sixteen hundred foot oval. The southern section was circular with an eight hundred foot diameter. There were two, 2 plus acre islands about one hundred to one hundred fifty feet to the west of the center where it pinched. The ten foot wide paved road ran from Anna's driveway to the other structure.

As Jules approached the narrowest point, there was a horizontal metal bar that blocked the path. The sign that hung from the crossbar stated: *'Don't even think of crossing—Big John'*. Jules laughed and got off the golf cart. She vaulted over the bar and walked to the unfinished structure. The beach house's design resembled Anna's, but without a second story, and looked like the roof was added as an afterthought.

Big John lay sprawled across the canvas bottom of a Hobie Cat drinking a Corona. He peeked under his dark shades as Jules approached. "I was wondering how long it would take you to snoop around the island."

"Is this where you live? Jules asked.

"Sometimes . . . this is Bucks house. He stopped construction when Char became vice president. Figured he wouldn't spend much time here. Then Anna decided to build her house and Buck figured he'd stay there. We talked him into finishing the first floor as a guest house. So yeah, I stay here and keep an eye on it when no one is using it. You should move in."

What and make your job easier, Jules thought. "Nah, I'm happy at Anna's for now. She's like my second mom, but it is a beautiful house. Maybe someday I'll move in."

"Hey, you wanna go for a ride?"

"Sure, but first . . . tell me what you know about the Anna and Char thing."

Big John choked on the beer in his mouth, and it spilled down the front of his T-shirt. "Grab yourself a beer."

Gotchya, Jules thought. "I don't drink alcohol, but thank you anyway—now spill the dirt, Big John."

Big John doffed his signature hat and rubbed his bald head. He jumped at the offer from Buck and Anna to protect Jules while she was on the island.

You're stalling, Jules thought, and gave him her pout look.

Big John must have caught on, because he began to spill the beans. "Okay, the way I see it, Buck and Char love each other deeply, but they also love their independence. Then Anna walked into their lives." Big John paused. "You are aware of the Miami caper, and how Anna was rescued?"

"Yeah, mom and Anna gave me the scoop."

"So. . . Buck and Char both fell in love with Anna."

Jules teeheed, and then placed her hands over her heart in an OMG moment.

"Don't make me explain that," begged Big John.

Jules flat out laughed. "Anna and mom gave me the low down on that, too. What do you know about the fake wedding?"

Big John pulled out a bandana and whipped his forehead. He gave Jules a questioning look.

"Anna and mom," she said. "Continue please."

"Good," Big John wiped his brow—relieved that he didn't have to explain. "So Char got what she always wanted—the presidency. The fake wedding shut up the detractors in DC. Anna got what she wanted, too, her own Nanoscience center. To Char and Anna, their jobs always came first, and Buck was caught in the middle."

"How so?" Jules asked.

"Buck hates DC. He likes SPI, but he loves Aspen and his mansion, Angel's Landing. So he takes assignments to keep himself on the move, and spends a lot of time at home."

"Fine," said Jules. "I'll let you off the hook."

"What's your concern?" Big John asked.

"I don't know. . . Char is great to me, and I like her a lot. But I love Anna."

"Everyone loves Anna," Big John said. "She will do anything for any of us."

"Is she all God and Country, like Buck?"

Big John laughed. "Don't tell anyone I said this, but I think Anna is God."

"Me, too. Now how about that ride."

For the next hour, Big John took Jules around the island, and pointed out the major sights. He showed her how to steer the Hobie, and Jules took over—she was a natural.

"Hey, if you really want to sail, Greg and I are taking the Hunter out this weekend."

Hum, Big John and the ex-spook are tight, I'll take advantage of that fact, too.. "What's a Hunter?" Jules asked.

"It's a fifty foot sailing palace. It has everything. I sleep on it a lot, too. We keep it docked at South Padre Island Fishing, about a mile south of here."

Jules checked the time on her R-CAT. "We'd better be getting back," she said. "I'm going to the gun range with Anna and Emma before the gadget demonstration tonight."

"Hey, anytime you want to take this out, you know where to find it."

"Thanks Big John. Hey, what do you think about the two missing girls?"

Big John's hat came off and out came the bandana again. Jules smiled. *Grandpa says the big guy isn't the sharpest tool in the shed, but there's nobody tougher or more loyal. Big John was known as the "Cooler of SPI"; everyone wanted him as a bouncer or bodyguard. Grandpa won, Big John joined The Corporation, and now he is my bodyguard.*

"Anna says it's not an issue."

"That's not what I asked," Jules said.

Big John's grin spread across his face. "What do you want me to do?"

Jules gave him a peck on the cheek. "That's better. I'd like you to check out the popular Spring Break hangouts, and see if anyone saw Sandy or Miffy."

"Who's Miffy?"

"Mary Francis Davenport, she went missing last night."

Jules knew that Big John had a smartphone that mirrored the R-CAT, but it didn't have any of the cool stuff, plus it only had one channel. "Let me see your phone." she said.

Big John handed it to her and she moved her phone over his. Big John's phone pinged, alerting him that he had a new text attachment. Jules opened it for him. "Show these two pictures to people you trust."

"How'd you do that?" Big John asked.

"Magic!"

The first thing Jules noted when she entered the gun range was the length. It was over three hundred yards, and definitely longer than the building. It extended out under the outside parking area. There were six shooter cubicles and behind the shooting area was a room with bulletproof glass that held the latest in exotic fire power.

On the wall by the door and in each booth were the rules and policies printed on a large placard. She also noted that there was no (RSO) ranger safety officer, whom she had seen at most of the ranges she visited with Grandpa and Jack. They were normally available to assist shooters and ensure the rules were followed. There was no one to monitor the mechanical ventilation and electronic systems either.

Bet BADDAY handled that, too.

The shooters were responsible for cleaning up their cubicle before they left; maintenance staff cleaned the rest of the range each morning.

The range was designed to GSA standards. The floors, walls, baffles, and bullet traps were built to dissipate the energy of the most powerful projectiles fired, and protect shooters from errant shots or misfires.

Anna and Emma were in the first two booths wearing eye and ear protection—per the rules. Jules watch as they each shot 9mm rounds at the popular B27 silhouette targets fifty feet away, with a five-and-a-half inch white bull's eye, and a one-inch black X in the center.

After they unloaded their fifteen round clips, they removed their protection, and pushed a button that sent their targets whirring back to them.

"Huh," Jules said. Both of them put all their rounds in the bull's eye, and Anna's target was missing the X in the middle. "Nice shooting Emma. I guess those things don't get in the way after all."

"Ha to you, too," Emma said. "Let's see what you got."

Anna and Emma stood behind Jules as she put a fresh silhouette on the target holder and ran the target out to seventy-five feet. She turned and winked at them as she put her eye and ear protection on. Jules took her stance and Anna set her stopwatch to zero. Anna timed her when Jules began to unload her fifteen round clip.

Nine seconds—not bad, thought Anna. "Let's see the target," Anna and Emma said in tandem.

Emma counted the holes—all in the bull's eye, and only the bottom half of the X was intact. "Do you sleep with that gun, too?"

Jules tried to imitate Buck's smile. "Nah, Grandpa Buck taught me well."

They each unloaded a couple of more clips before Anna called it time. "Clean up and let's go. We have a demonstration to get to."

10

SPI Advance Nanoscience Research Center
Thursday Night April 4th

Psychopaths by nature were extremely manipulative and could easily gain people's trust. They learn to mimic emotions, and despite their inability to actually feel them, they would appear normal to unsuspecting people. Psychopaths were often well educated and held steady jobs. Tony Labarbera was an exception to that rule. He may have had a steady job; he worked for the cleaning company that was contracted to vacuum the carpets at the research center once a week. But with multiple personalities, and an IQ barely higher than the seventy-two degrees that the computerized HVAC system was set at, Tony was just plum loco.

From the second story window of the South Padre Island Advanced Nanoscience Research Center, Tony Labarbera was glued to the window.

Aha . . . the rich bitch blonde with the red Ferrari.

He leered at Jules as she sat in the car. His eyes never left her as she hopped out, and got behind the seat of a more undignified ride. His scowl deepened as he watched her direct a golf cart over the bridge from the private island.

As Jules approached the research center, Tony fell into his *gangsta* persona.

Um um good, I got me a lil somethin' somethin' goin' down. His hand moved to the front to his pants. *Gonna crush down on dat.*

"Yo, check out the body on that bitch," he said to no one in particular. He thought he had the floor to himself.

"What a perv!" said the woman passing a few feet behind him, who obviously caught his whole act.

"Sorry ma'am, it was nothin'. . . stubbed my toe." He looked around to make sure he was alone this time, and started to touch himself again. "I'm gonna have that," he said. "Soon as I'm done having fun with the one I have back at the dump." He didn't give Sandy a second thought.

The dump was the trailer he had at the South Padre Island KOA, just south of Route 100, where he lived. Tony had no problem picking up chicks, as long as he didn't fall into his *gangsta* persona. He had that tall, dark, and handsome look that appealed to most women. Spring Break quenched his thirst for sex with the gaggle of high school and colleges girls that got piss drunk, and had the motto: what happens on South Padre, stays on South Padre.

When Spring Break was over, it was back to Matamoros, Mexico for good old twenty-five cent hookers.

Dr. Bryce Kellogg watched with amazed interest from the other end of the hallway as Tony continued his lewd act. His attention was not directed at the extremely beautiful Dr. Semyonova, or the well stacked and equally gorgeous Dr. Dash. No. Tony's performance was aimed at sixteen year old Jules Spenser.

Dr. Kellogg would not be attending the demonstration tonight; she had other plans, but she was interested in the members of the Alphabet Soup community who *were* attending. She watched as the Director of Homeland Security Micky Livingston, and the Director of the CIA Snowdan Jones, finished their cigars while a gaggle of secret service agents dressed like the Blues Brother looked on.

Five minutes later the Director of the NSA (National Security Agency) arrived, she couldn't remember his name, but she knew who he was. She gave it ten more minutes and passed through security to leave the building.

As she walked out the front door to the facility, a black non-descript Tahoe pulled to the curb. Two linebacker size men in suits exited the SUV with Glock's drawn, and scanned the immediate area.

Then one of the men gave a signal by twirling his index finger in the air. A few seconds later, a drop dead gorgeous woman in designer glasses, and a form fitting body suit exited the Tahoe. She was immediate surrounded by the two men, who then escorted her to the front door.

I'll be damned, thought Bryce Kellogg. *The President of the United States is here incognito.*

Bryce Kellogg was not rich, but she was a genius. She had a PhD in Materials Science and Engineering from the University of Tennessee, and no laboratory on earth had the equipment that was available to her at the SPI research center. After numerous requests, she was hired to the academic professorial staff. She had access to all the equipment at the research center, and would lecture the students on advanced biopolymer-based nanostructures, electrically conductive transparent films and flexible photovoltaic—a requirement of all touchscreen gadgets.

But in her spare time, she continued her research in quantum electrodynamics, and electromagnetic radiation. Bryce was very familiar with Faraday's Law predicting how a magnetic field would interact with an electric circuit to produce an electromotive force (EMF)—a phenomenon called electromagnetic induction. She also knew that the research center had a sophisticated Faraday Shield that blocked external static and non-static electrical fields. It protected the electronic equipment from lightning and electrostatic discharges, as well as protecting research and development from prying ears and eyes.

Although EMP (Electro Magnetic Pulse) weapons were globally outlawed, that did not stop terrorists from building them. EMP's with a simple modification of radar could bounce pulses of energy off aircrafts, vehicles, and other objects to fry there electronics. Non-nuclear EMP weapons had the potential to devastate the electronic systems of areas as large as a city or as small as a selected object, without being seen, heard, or felt by anyone. The research center had its own division that made daily advances against the war on terror—Bryce was a member of that group.

Bryce moved to America with her mother when she was eight. This was soon after her father had committed suicide. Her father was a brilliant Quantum Physicist who was making advancements in biopolymer structures. When funds became tight, he partnered with two not so brilliant, but very rich physicists. When he created what would become the first touch screen device. His partners stole the plans and created a patent in their own names. They became richer and with their financial stature, started rumors about her father. The other two scientists, with the help of their shyster lawyers, dissolved the partnership. Her father was left broke and ruined.

He felt the only option left to him was to put a gun to his head.

With the insurance money from her father's death, Bryce and her mother moved to America to begin a new life. They applied for, and were granted citizenship, under the name Kellogg.

Three weeks earlier she was dining at Louie's Backyard. Bryce was immersed in her father's papers, when the waiter placed a bottle of Dom Perignon 1996 on her table and stunned her.

"I didn't order that," she said.

The waiter smiled. "Compliments of an admirer," he said, as he began to pour the nectar of Gods into a fluted Champaign glass.

Bryce took a sip.

Ten seconds later, heads turned as a stunning brunette in a black cocktail dress made her way across the restaurant. Her waist length hair—worthy of a Pantene commercial—bounced with each step. She smiled and flashed her piercing brown eyes at each acknowledgement of her beauty, until she appeared at Bryce's table.

"Bryce?"

"OMG. Kala?"

"Yes my dear friend," said Kala Kellingworth. "How do you like the wine?"

"I think it's called Champaign."

Kala smiled at her friend's naivety, and sat down across from her.

Bryce and Kala small talked about their youthful days as best friends, and then moved on to their days as roommates in college. Bryce was well aware that Kala came from money—old rich as they called it.

"So what brings you to South Padre Island?" Bryce asked.

"My daddy just bought the Seabreeze III Resort as an investment," she said. "And I just happen to have a three bedroom penthouse suite there."

"I'd love to see it," Bryce said.

"Where are you staying?" Kala asked.

"I have a one bedroom suite on the campus of the South Padre Island Advance Nanoscience Research Center."

Kala smiled again while she searched deep into her friend's eyes. "Come see my suite, and if you like it, you can move in. Hey, it will be just like college."

Kala thought about the offer. "Okay, let's go see it, but no promises." She waved for her waiter.

"Check please."

The waiter looked to Kala, and then at Bryce. "Ms. Kellingworth has already paid your tab ma'am."

Kala's penthouse suite comprised the entire twenty-fourth floor of the Seabreeze III Resort, and had unimpeded views of the entire island. Bryce was impressed. She and Kala began where they left off at Louie's. At eleven o'clock, Bryce called it a night.

"So . . . what do you think?" Kala said.

"It's beautiful."

"That's not what I mean," Kala said, and smiled. "Do you want to stay here?"

"Maybe on the weekends, when I'm free. I have a tough schedule at the research center, and need my sleep. Besides, I can be in my office in five minutes."

"Good. It's settled. You can move in this weekend," Kala said. "I have a demanding schedule, too."

Bryce broke out in laughter. "What? Travelling the globe."

"Just so happens, yes. I leave in a few weeks for Las Lenas, Argentina for four weeks of back bowl helicopter skiing."

"Figures. Listen, dear, I have to go home and get ready for tomorrow."

They both hugged, and as Bryce walked to the door Kala grabbed her arm. "Here take this. It's your key to the room and elevator. Only that card has access to the penthouse floor."

Bryce took the key, and kissed her friend on the cheek. "Love you. See you Friday night."

"Your room will be waiting for you," Kala said, as the door to the elevator closed.

Bryce mused about the idea of moving in while the elevator dinged at each floor she passed. She liked the idea of being away from the prying eyes and ears of the facility staff, and especially, BADDAY the super computer that protected the research facility like a new born baby. With Kala away for a few weeks, the idea sounded even better. She could come and go as she pleased without having to explain herself.

A second thought occurred to her, they were the same size, and Kala had an awesome array of clothing. Maybe it's time for some experimentation with the night life of South Padre Island.

GENE HILGREEN

11

SPI Advance Nanoscience Research Center
Thursday Night April 4th

Jules followed Anna and Emma down the hall to the auditorium at the north end of the second floor. She thought about how well she shot at the range, and how much better Anna was at shooting.

Is there anything that woman can't do. Damn, she thought, *even super rack Emma shoots better than me.*

Jules caught the stare from the good looking guy, who shut down his machine as they passed. He was the kind of guy who belonged on the cover of a romance novel—tall, athletic, wavy dark hair, and a tan to die for. He didn't belong in a tee shirt and white coveralls. *What am I thinking? He's probably staring at Anna and Emma—surely not me.*

"Hey, Anna," Jules said when she caught up to her. "Who's the hottie in the coveralls?"

Anna continued her pace, and without looking at Jules, replied, "SPI Carpet Cleaning. And no fraternization with the hired help, young lady."

Jules cocked her head over her shoulder for one more look at Mr. Hottie. The man's stance never changed; he was still checking them out. When he caught Jules looking, he winked. His smile turned from chaste to raunchy as his hand moved to the front of his coveralls. Jules quickly turned away as a chill rifled through her body.

The auditorium, which sat one-hundred-twenty plus people, had a raised stage where presentations or demonstrations could be performed with an unimpeded view. Jules could see DDHS Livingston and DCI Jones front and center. The two seats on each side of them were empty. Roy, who was standing in front of them, motioned for Jules to take one of the seats. On the stage was a table with an arraignment of gadgets. Next to the table were life-like robots: a panther, a snow leopard, and a deer.

As Anna, Roy, and Emma climbed the stairs to the stage, the lights dimmed. The double doors to the auditorium opened and three people quietly entered—choosing to sit in the last row. Anna approached the dais and opened her notebook. When she took in the audience, she smiled.

"As some of you are aware, this research facility and school had always been a dream of mine. Its fruition and realization was only made possible by my best friend and biggest donor, Dr. Charlotte "Char" Vice-Davidssen." Tears began to accumulate in Anna's eyes, "Madame President, would you please join me, and open this ceremony."

Nobody knew that Char was coming except Whitecloud and Priest. She wanted to surprise Anna, and she had a special gift that she wanted to give to Jules in person. Char was concerned that she was losing Jules. Not that Jules liked Anna better—that was expected—it's just that Jules stopped confiding with her like she used too.

Besides, Char had the best protection on earth. Buck was not pleased—to put it nicely—when she demanded Whitecloud and Priest's protection while she was President of the United States.

Gunny gave Char a heads-up that Jules wanted to learn to fly the Hughes. There would be a brand new one waiting for her when she got her license.

All eyes turned to the back of the room. The President of the United States stood and walked to the front with her two bodyguards. James 'Whitecloud' White and Ronny 'Priest' Crowe stood on either side of her, and cleared the way as supporters reached out for handshakes, or just a chance to touch her.

Whitecloud and Priest were not Secret Service; they were members of The Corporation, and had fought side by side with Buck Davidssen and Jack Mameli in the US Marine Corps. Char sat down next to Jules, and gave her a kiss. Whitecloud and Priest nodded to the DDHS and DCI, and then stood off to the side. Around the room were several members of the Secret Service and CIA, but they were not on the presidential security detail.

Sporting a light gray Vika leather jacket and pant suit, the face of an angel, drop dead gorgeous shape, stunning cobalt blue eyes, and her platinum hair in a ponytail— Char could have easily passed for a model—not the president of the United States. A tear had formed in her eye, too when she smiled up toward Anna. "No, Anna . . . this is your show."

A gasp or two were heard through the crowd when Char winked at Anna.

Anna winked back. The exchange did not go unnoticed by Jules. And then Anna began:

"As the leader in nanotechnology research and its application, we have developed a completely new set of building blocks that is based on nanoparticles and DNA. Instead of taking what nature gives us, we can control every property of the new material we make. We've always had this vision of building matter and controlling architecture from the bottom up, and now we've proved it can be done.

"New materials developed using his method have improved the efficiency of optics, electronics, and energy storage technologies. These same nanoparticle building blocks have already found wide-spread commercial utility in biology and medicine as diagnostic probes for markers of disease. Our research has moved to the cellular level by creating micro particles that can be programmed to shut down the genetic production line that cranks out disease-related proteins. In laboratory tests, these newly created "nanorobots" all but eradicated basic virus infection.

"We have built nanobots that rebuild tissue molecules in order to close a wound, or rebuild the walls of veins and arteries to stop bleeding and save lives. They could make their way through the bloodstream to the heart and perform heart surgery molecule by molecule without many of the risks and discomfort associated with traditional open-heart operations.

"With additional funding, we hope to build nanorobots that will have many miraculous effects on brain research, and cancer research for finding cures for leukemia and AIDS."

For the next hour and a half Anna, Roy, and Emma demonstrated the devices and robots. She fielded questions for another half hour and ended the demo a few minutes after eight p.m.

Jules helped Roy and Jai pack up all the gadgets. Roy had held four devices to the side.

"Dr. Singh, what are those devices?" Jules asked.

Roy studied Jules's expression. "These are the new GPS/IPS jammers we are working on in the nano lab. They are for our three favorite donors, Char, Micky, and Snowdan."

"Who's the fourth for?" Jules inquired.

"I'm going to demo it later at Anna's."

Jules looked in the gadget box and didn't see anymore. *I'd sure like to get my hands on one of them.*

When all the robots and devices were put back in the lab, Jules and Roy joined the group standing outside of the auditorium. Jai went back to his dorm.

After hugs and kisses, Micky said, "Well I had wanted to take you all out to dinner, but with the boss here, I'll leave it up to Char."

Char laughed. "I called Big John half an hour ago. I told him to get the barbeque going with the a-list food order for thirty people. We'll enjoy ourselves at Anna's." She winked at DDHS Micky Livingston and DCI Snowdan Jones. "This way the boys can smoke their cigars without getting us arrested."

Because she didn't want to cause press speculation, Char flew in on her private jet instead of Air Force One. She had planned to stay until Saturday for Jules's birthday. Then she was going to head for Aspen and Angel's

Landing. She would stay at Anna's house, while Whitecloud and Priest would stay with Big John at the unfinished guesthouse. Micky and Snowdan planned on staying a few more days and got rooms at a nearby hotel for themselves and their security detail.

Roy demonstrated the newly designed GPS/IPS jammer against an array of gadgets that Micky Livingston and Snowdan Jones brought along with them. The device jammed every communication device, and the top two American spies were impressed. Jules was equally impressed, and her mind that worked in ones and zeros was already churning with how she could tweak it a tad more. Maybe even catch BADDAY napping.

Jax and Ramsey kissed their daughter goodnight at eleven and left for the hotel. Anna gave last call at the Tiki bar at midnight. The smiles on Micky and Snowdan's face showed they were happy to steal some time from Washington DC to catch the demonstration, after which they rounded up their teams and left. Whitecloud and Priest, who had switched to coffee at ten, drove around the little island on golf carts with Big John, Roy, and Jules.

"Hey Jules, is the *Genius* taking care of you?" Whitecloud asked.

Jules giggled. "You have to be a little more specific, Whitecloud. Everyone on campus is a genius."

"Sorry, you're right. See, we've known Roy . . . well . . . since back when he was the only genius around."

Roy offered, "Genius is my *code name*."

"Jules, have you settled on a code name yet?" Priest asked. "You better pick one before Anna does."

"I'm going with *Parker*," Jules said. "Knowing Roy and Anna . . . they will code name me *Psycho* or *Socially Inept*."

"Jules, we would never do that," Roy said.

"I like it—Parker it is," Whitecloud said, and then laughed. "Just like that chick from *Leverage*."

"Yup—that's me—twenty pounds of crazy in a five pound bag."

Everyone had a good laugh, including Jules. Satisfied that the island was safe, they drove back to Anna's and returned Jules.

Anna and Char were on the deck waiting. "

I picked Parker," Jules said.

"For what?" they echoed.

"My code name," she said, and then kissed them both goodnight and headed for her room.

"What was that all about, guys?" Char had aimed the question at Whitecloud, Priest, and Roy.

"Let me take this," Roy said. "The topic of code names came up, and genius junior came up with *Parker* before someone chose one for her."

"Goodnight, guys," Char said.

"Island's safe and sound," Whitecloud said. They all said their goodnights and headed out.

Jules, meanwhile—content and happy with herself—fell asleep with her R-CAT in her hand.

12

North of Island Adventure Park
Friday morning April 5th

Musty air barely trickled through the clogged filter of the air conditioner. The noise that emanated from it reminded Tony of a clothes drier with a pair of sneakers rattling around inside. The slight movement of ribbons that hung from the equally filthy vents told him it was still working. The dank air cooled the trailer enough to make it bearable.

Tony stirred, and with a gasp, pulled himself from the grip of his nightmare. *Why am I sweating?* His hands clawed at his crust caked eyes, and then he wiped away the beads that covered his forehead. His dreams were the same every night: women from his past continuously passed him by— recounting their last seconds on earth. He couldn't control his dreams, and when he was awake, he couldn't get the girl with the red Ferrari out of his mind—he was obsessed. No other female ever made him feel like this. He had to have her.

The LED clock on the wall flashed 3:55. His body begged for more sleep, unaware that today would be a long and demanding day. He instinctively knew, even if his body didn't.

Tony's eyes scanned the compact trailer from the lumpy couch he slept on to the bed where Miffy was tied up. A ragged blanket covered most of her torso. She was still knocked out from the drugs he'd shot into her. He got excited watching her large breasts rise and fall. He kept her in a perpetual buzz. He didn't care if the body moved, he just wanted a hot body, and Miffy had a hot body.

She just wasn't the girl in the red Ferrari.

"Screw it," he said, as he ogled at her. "No—I'll screw her."

Tony kept the company van at his trailer that night. His boss told him to be at the research center by six a.m. to redo the carpets. No problem, he thought, *another day close to my dream girl.*

He would rid himself of Miffy in the barren dunes before he went in to work. *Piece of cake,* he thought. *And no more distractions.* He rubbed himself just thinking about it. *Why not?* Tony pulled the blanket away from her. He'd decided to go out with a bang. Miffy uttered incoherently when he saddled in. During his lustful, vile act, she came out of her stupor and began screaming. With her arms and legs tied spread eagle, there was nothing she could do.

"Why are you doing this to me?"

"My little hobby keeps me in checks—get the pun," he said while pounding away. "Money bitch."

She spit in his face.

He savagely smacked her face, and then continued defiling her.

"I'll get you more money."

He moved his face closer to her. "It's not about the money, it never really was. It's about power."

She snapped her head upward and tried to bite his nose off. He smacked her again, and grabbed some duct tape off the nightstand—taping her mouth shut.

"Now I have to start over, bitch." He made her pay for her act of defiance, only stopping once he was spent.

Exhausted and satisfied, he got off of her and pulled up his pants. A lecherous smile spread across his face when he admired the pile of cash and jewelry on his table. He had accumulated that little treasure trove over the past few weeks, and would be sitting pretty for a while.

Tony looked back at Miffy. "My hobby is a powerful thing. I can't describe it, but I like it."

Tears ran down Miffy's cheeks.

"Po-wer," Tony said, accenting each syllable. "Go ahead, bitch, and cry your ass off."

Miffy eyed him severely, and then broke off her stare. She turned her head away from him and cried.

He shot Miffy up with another dose of Special K—he was done with her. He didn't care if the dose was lethal. He gathered her clothes and her empty Louis Vuitton shoulder strap bag. He thought about selling that, too, but thought better of it and threw it in the garbage bag with the clothes.

He poked his head out the trailer door. Sunrise loomed hours away, and nothing stirred in the trailer park. He threw her over his shoulder, grabbed the garbage bag, and dumped both in the back of the van. He knew the perfect place to dispose of his trash, having scouted out several isolated spots during the week.

Tony was not as alone as he had thought; he was shadowed again this night. The figure tailed Tony at a safe distance—not that it mattered—the shadow knew Tony was an idiot. The shadow watched as he dumped the body in the dunes.

After Tony was gone, the figure smiled when the moonlight glimmered across the dune, giving clues to the whereabouts of the buried body. This person was special, and the stalker had momentous plans for her. But tonight, the first step to the grand plan would unfold. And that first step would be the staging of Sandy's body.

It didn't take long for the shadow to figure out that Jules Spenser, the Wunderkind and protégé of Dr. Anna

Semyonova, was Tony's next target. Knowing Tony's thirst for beautiful rich girls and stalking him the same way he stalked his prey; the shadowy individual knew it wouldn't be long before Tony made his move.

A surprise would be left for both of them.

The dark figure drove along the shore line to where the highway ended. Having tailed Tony and Jules for days, the person knew this particular stretch of land was of interest to both of them.

A beguiling pool of luminous light splashed off the gulf and lit up the beach. The individual followed the brilliant source of light out into the sea toward the full moon—that was when it became apparent.

A flag on a pole stuck in the middle of a sandbar waved in the distance.

The figure stripped Sandy naked, and placed the clothes in a bag—these would come in handy later. With Sandy's naked body in a fireman's carry and a surfboard under the other arm—the stalker wadded out into the gulf, secured Sandy to the board, and paddled out to the flag.

Printed across the flag were two words: Jules Island.

Could this get any better?

The shadow laid out Sandy in a pose—her hand wrapped around the flag pole. Satisfied with the display, the individual paddled back to shore on the surfboard.

GENE HILGREEN

13

Anna's Island
Friday April 5th

The R-CAT buzzed in Jules' hand at a quarter to five. Her t-shirt and panties had yet to hit the floor as she adjusted the straps of her Speedo Proback swimsuit in place. Jules was out of her bedroom, down the stairs, and in Anna's immaculate kitchen pouring a cup of coffee to go by five. As she passed by the Tiki bar on her way to the Ferrari, she saw the box that held Roy's demo jammer and stopped in her tracks. Curiosity took over, and she opened the box expecting to see nothing but bubble wrap. Surprised that the jammer was in the box, she slipped it in her backpack and tossed the box in the garbage can.

—Roy must have gotten caught up with the guys and forgotten about it. I'll do my own demo when I get to Jules Island.

She fired up the Ferrari electronically, letting it purr. She slowly took it out of the driveway, not wanting to wake up Anna. Today she was not racing; her focus would be on her surroundings. She plugged her R-CAT into the adapter and listened to her messages. She had a message and a couple of attachments from BADDAY.

The first two days she was so locked in on the road and the *final mile* sign that she never saw the sign for Island Adventure Park to her left. She had read about it in one of the brochures at Anna's house. Island Adventure Park offered ATV and horseback riding trails—it also had a petting zoo. She made a mental note to stop there on the way back.

When Jules reached the end of Ocean Boulevard (State Park Road 100) she saw a beachcomber walking along the shoreline. She didn't give him a second thought as she opened the first attachment from BADDAY.

It contained an analysis of all the sights where a video camera as well as the photos her mom had taken that had Sandy in them. It also included the names of the people that were also caught within the pictures and video frames. There weren't many photos or video sequences, but several names showed up more than once, and one of them was Gunther Baader. Jules opened the second attachment. It included the actual photos and videos. She was so concerned with the shots of Gunther; she didn't give a second thought to the four other girls, nor the handsome looking guy with the dark wavy hair and deep brown eyes.

Satisfied that Gunther was her prime suspect, Jules shut down the Ferrari and took to the gulf for her morning swim. As she approached the shore line a beachcomber was looking out toward her private little sand bar through binoculars. Jules smiled as she got closer. The man was six foot plus, his long grayish blond hair was tied back and covered over by an old military bush hat. He wore cut-off jeans and had a fiftieth reunion tie dye Woodstock shirt on that appeared fairly new. When he turned toward Jules, his piercing blue eyes took her aback.

Mom would love this guy, she thought. "Hi y'all, my name is Jules. See anything interesting?"

The beachcomber lowered his binoculars and turned toward Jules with an extended hand. "Hi y'all right back at ya," he said, and then added. "Name's Gene, but my friends call me the Mayor."

"Well, Mayor, anything interesting?"

"Looks like you have some company today on your little island."

Jules cocked her head and gave the Mayor the evil eye. "Been spying on me have you?"

The Mayor laughed. "No, no my dear, but the Mayor sees and hears all."

Jules secured her R-CAT into a waterproof pack she wrapped around her ankle. "Well Mayor, let's see who my guest is."

"No, you go on," he said. "I have to get back and open up the Island Adventure Park. Listen, stop by anytime and I'll set you up with an ATV on the house."

"That's a deal, Mayor." With that she ran into the water, dove head first into a large breaker, and swam for her little island. The sand bar fluctuated with the tides, and was no more than thirty feet wide today. Smack in the middle was a naked girl. Jules looked back toward the shore, but the Mayor was long gone.

"Hey, are you all right," she yelled, but got no response back. With each step toward the naked girl, Jules knew she was *not only* not all right, but dead. She pulled out her R-CAT and snapped pictures from every angle. Although she commanded BADDAY to run a search, she already knew who the dead girl was. After getting confirmation, she immediately hit the button to call Anna.

Twenty minutes later, Anna arrived and made her way to the sand bar.

"What took you so long?" Jules inquired.

Anna ripped off a sentence in Russian as she climbed the sand bar. Jules ignored it. She loved Anna, and knew she wasn't big on apologies. That's because in her universe, Anna was never wrong.

"Hey, I got here as soon as I could," Anna finally said, stretching out the word *could* so it sounded more like *back off* than *I'm sorry*.

Jules looked up at her briefly then back toward Sandy. Anna's demeanor bore a haggard feel—something else was bothering her. It was almost impossible for Anna not to look anything but beautiful. Jules let her abruptness go and instead said evenly, "Dr. Anna Semyonova, meet Sandy Russell."

Anna knelt down next to Jules and gave her a hug. "I'm sorry, honey; I should have trusted your instinct."

Jules hugged her back and kissed her cheek. That *I'm sorry* actually sounded sincere.

Anna studied the question in Jules' eyes. "Honey, this isn't a coincidence. The killer is trying to talk to someone, and the flag tells me it's you."

For the briefest moment Jules turned into a kid and let out a pout, which she sucked in almost immediately, gaining control of herself.

Anna held her tight. "No more late night or early morning swims alone, until this person is caught."

"Anna, I think I know who the killer is."

"Vat—"

The exchange caused Jules to laugh. Everything after 'Vat' was in Russian. Not having studied Russian, Jules was left to surmise that most everything after "Vat" was sure to be filled with curse words. "I love it when you talk dirty." Jules said, and started giggling.

"Something else has come up," Anna said. "We'll talk when we get home, but first let me call Chief Smith at SPIPD."

Jules's mind was elsewhere on the ride back home. She caught the Mayor in front of the Island Adventure Park sign in her rear view mirror. He was waving at her. She extended her arm through the open roof top and waved back. She turned her lips up in a brief smile and nodded to herself. She had the feeling she would be seeing more of the Mayor.

Her attention back on the road, she floored the Ferrari and beat Anna home by a good minute. Jack Mameli and Dr. Emma Dash were standing on the front deck when she pulled up to the garage.

Jules knew something was amiss from the look on Jack's face. Jack was Buck's best friend and was supposed to be with him on the mission. Jack must have come in very early this morning.

"Where's Grandpa Buck?" Jules screamed as she ran toward the deck, tears pouring from both eyes.

Jack put his hands up to slow her down, and then pulled her in, hugging her tight. "He's fine honey, just a couple of more dings in his suit of armor."

"How dinged, and where is he Jack?" Jules manage between sniffles.

"He's at—"

"Angel's Landing," said Char as she burst through the front door between Whitecloud and Priest. "Jules, we have to talk." Char paused as Anna pulled up to the garage. She slammed on the breaks sending sand spewing in every direction. Wrenching the truck's door open she took off at a run toward Jules, her truck still idling.

Jules turned toward Anna and caught her in an embrace. Anna hugged her hard, ran her hands through her hair, trying to calm her down.

Jules pulled from the embraced and stared at Char. "How bad is Buck?"

Char came right out with it. "He got shot in the thigh. He's fine, but needs to stay off his feet for a couple weeks."

"I want to go see him!" Jules ordered.

Anna pulled her inside her arms again. "Honey, you need to stay here. Jack and Emma will watch you while I'm gone. Jack has already called in additional security for the facility and the island, and I'm assigning Big John as your personal bodyguard. I'll call him before I leave.

"But—"

"Listen honey, I called Chief Smith, and told him my concerns. He assured me that Sandy's case would take precedence. Sandy's parents are on their yacht in the Mediterranean off the coast of Spain. They won't be here for several days—"

"But—"

"Jules! Stop! Char and I are leaving in an hour," she looked toward Char and Jack—they nodded their confirmation. "It's a national security matter. That's all I can say right now. I will be back in a couple of days. Buck will come here when he's ready to travel. You will be safe

119

here. Jack has everything under control. Think of the rest of the students."

Whitecloud and Priest, who were loading the Tahoe with luggage, returned as Jules started to interrupt Anna again. "Hey Parker, listen to Anna. No one is better than Jack—you're safe here."

Jules sighed, she knew they were right—nobody was better than Jack, and she had Big John, too. "What are you going to tell Mom?"

"That I have to go to DC with Char," Anna said.

"Oh, I get it. This is one of those *'Don't tell mom'* moments." Jules said, and for emphasis she held up both of her hands forming *'air quotes'*.

"Yes," said Anna and Char in tandem.

Anna continued. "Think about it. What would your mom say if she found out you were at Angel's Landing, and not here."

"Fine then. I'm going to class," Jules said, as she brushed by Char and her entourage, to run up the steps to her room. She slammed her door for effect. It was six-thirty. Char and Anna would be gone by seven-thirty give or take. She hit the icon on her R-CAT for Big John.

"Yo," said Big John after five rings. "What can I do for you at this ungodly hour?"

Jules laughed. "It's almost seven big guy, shouldn't you be up getting the bar ready or something."

Big John let out a big Texas hoot. "Seven my ass! Okay, you got me. What's up?"

Jules cut to the chase. "Did you hear about what happen to Grandpa Buck?"

"No," Big John said, and paused sounding surprised. "Should I have?"

Jules caught the surprised sound in his voice. "No, it's ok. He just got dinged up. Listen Anna is leaving in an hour for Angel's Landing with Char, she's going to assign you to watch over me."

"I always watch over you."

"Yeah, I know. Listen, I have some recon work for you."

"I'm listening."

"Meet me at the Hobbie Cat at 0800 we're going for a ride," Jules said, then added. "What do you know about the Mayor?"

"Huh."

"Gene," Jules said. "The Mayor."

"Oh. . . Gene H. We go way back. Nothing happens on SPI without him hearing about it."

"Just what I wanted to hear," Jules said and let out a sly laugh. "We're going to pay him a visit."

GENE HILGREEN

14

Isla Blanca Trailer Park
Friday April 5th

After dumping Miffy, Tony Labarbera needed to wake up, and decided to head home for a quick shower before going to work. He could be at the research center in five minutes at this time of day, and let the spray pound on him for fifteen minutes.

Feeling content and alive, Tony had an extra bounce in his step as he sashayed to the front door of his trailer. The news that blurted from his police scanner—another hobby—stopped him dead in his tracks. A missing person found dead; the location was the end of State Road 100— Ocean Boulevard.

Couldn't be, thought Tony. *Must be someone else.*

Someone had in fact found Sandy's body, and called it in. What Tony didn't know was that the layers of lead sheets he stole from a construction site to patch up his trailer roof made him impregnable to BADDAY's GPS and IPS scans. Sandy and Miffy's phone and location had gone undetected from BADDAY, and the local authorities.

He decided to take a quick run by the scene. It wasn't where he dumped the body. When he arrived at the end of Ocean Boulevard, the area was already roped off with SPI's finest securing the scene. Local news crews were bellying up to the ropes, screaming for reports, and filming anything that seemed worthwhile to broadcast on the eight o'clock morning news.

Tony scanned the crowd of gawkers looking for the bitch with the red Ferrari. She wasn't there. He zoomed in on the scene with his binoculars. What he saw next sent chills through his body. Police were walking around the sand dune with the flag on it, and the girl they had on the stretcher was definitely Sandy.

Something was not right, Tony thought. *There's no way the body could have gotten there—unless someone moved it.* Trying to maintain his cool, he left for the research center. Security would show him arriving at ten after six.

"I've seen this guy around the island," the Mayor said, and handed the pictures back to Jules. He then turned toward Big John. "I believe he has a trailer in the park where your old bag of bones is rotting away."

Big John had called ahead, and Mayor Gene had met them at the dock on the bay side of Island Adventure Park with an ATV for him and Jules.

Big John revved his ATV, and turned to face Jules. "Told ya. The Mayor sees all."

Jules nodded at the Mayor and gave her ATV a couple of revs, too. "BADDAY says he works for SPI Carpet Cleaning, and has a PO Box here on SPI as a mailing address."

"Sorry Jules, but SPI doesn't have mail delivery," said the Mayor. "But I'm sure he resides in that trailer park—"

"No biggie," Jules interrupted. "He's not my prime suspect, but I would like to put a tail on him anyway."

The Mayor leaned forward on his ATV and stared straight at Jules. His piercing eyes expressed his seriousness. "Jules...even us dumb, ol' Texans read the newspaper now and again. I recognized you that first day on the beach, Miss National Champion...so tell me why you're getting involved in this murder mystery?"

Big John jumped in. "Mayor, Jules isn't just a champion gymnast, she's Buck Davidssen's granddaughter, and also a prodigy—"

"I read that, too, Big John, but—"

Jules put her hands up and the Mayor stopped mid-sentence. "Tell me what you know about the Corporation."

The Mayor looked toward Big John and he nodded. "Okay then, I've seen your Grandfather and his military types around the Science Center, and I've seen him with that old CIA spook who lives near Blackbeard's, but other than that . . . not much."

Jules thought he knew more than he was saying, because she knew Big John was a talker. "Fine then," she said. "I have the best spy system on earth at my disposal, not to mention my grandpa's team of Snake Eaters, but—and this is a big but—I want to do this on my own." She looked back and forth between the two men. "I want you two on my team."

"This could get ugly, young lady," the Mayor said.

Jules pulled her Glock-26 from her backpack. "Did Big John happen to mention that I'm a marksman, too?" The Mayor's eyes lit up. "Didn't think so," she said.

"What's the plan?" said the Mayor.

Jules beamed ear to ear. "There's a party at Louie's tonight. Big John will shadow me. I'd like you to see if this guy," Jules held up the photo of Tony Labarbera, "shows up at the Phish concert, and tail him." Jules handed the Mayor a smart phone. "Just press one to get me." Jules saw the twenty-one foot Mako fishing boat with 'The Mayor' printed across the rear at the dock when they pulled in. "Can you get that to Big John's dock?" she asked, pointing at the boat.

"I can get her anywhere on the island," said the Mayor.

"Good, we'll meet up later," Jules said. "But right now I have to get to class, and spy on my favorite suspect."

Gunther plopped down at his workstation and saw that Jai was alone today. "How's your girlfriend doing?" he asked.

"My girlfriend? What the hell are you talking about?" Jai snapped.

"Hey, no offense. I saw the news this morning; big shot prez was in town."

Jai ignored him, he wasn't invited back to Anna's house after the demo.

"So, how's your babe doing?" Gunther said

"My babe?" Jai repeated. "My lab partner is doing . . . turn around, and mind your own damn business Gunther . . . that's how she's doing."

Jules was running late, but so was Dr. Emma Dash. Jules entered the lab just in time to catch the tail end of the discussion.

Gunther slinked down in his seat, and didn't say another word.

Jules leaned over toward Jai. "What was that all about?"

"Nothing . . . just Gunther being an ass," he said. "Hey listen, I can't make the class party tonight, I have to help Uncle Roy with a new project."

"Just make sure you're free for my birthday surprise party," she winked. "I have to work tonight, too."

When Emma walked through the door all eyes turned to her. She walked straight to the front of the class. "I'm sorry, but this class is cancelled today. For those that wish to attend, Dr. Singh is demonstrating new equipment in the auditorium. Otherwise have a nice weekend."

Jules and Jai rose to leave.

"Jules, can I speak with you a moment in private," Emma said.

Jai nodded. "I'm headed to the auditorium. Call me later if you get a chance."

Jules nodded, and followed Emma.

"Jules, Anna is worried about you and wants Jack and me to keep an eye on you." Emma turned her hands up in surrender. She was looking for a response from Jules, but didn't receive anything. "So no funny business, and make sure someone is with you tonight." She made air quotes, bending her fingers, "get it?"

Jules gave her patented smile. "No worries Emma, Big John is my bodyguard tonight." She then gave Emma a satisfied smirk and turned to leave, but she couldn't resist imitating Emma and air mailed air quotes right back at her. "Get it?"

"Jack would like it if you had dinner tonight with us."

"When?"

"1800," Emma said, and smiled.

"So Doctor Hottie has a thing for Jack," Jules said. Before turning to leave, she added. "Jack likes that military talk. Tell him I'll be there."

Gunther stood a few steps outside the doorway, and blocked Jules's exit. He grabbed for her arm. "What's the deal?"

Jules tried to pull away from his grip.

"And what's Jai's problem?" he said in a snotty, condescending manner. "Is he like that with everybody?"

"No," Jules said, removing his hand, and twisting it— dropping Gunther to his knees. "Just child molesters and assholes. Have a nice day."

Louie's lived up to its reputation; the music was great and loud, but Jules was disappointed. At ten o'clock she decided to call it a night. No Gunther, and no Tony. She called the Mayor for an update, and he reported the same thing.

Big John downed his beer. "Jules, you want anything for the ride home?"

"Yeah, get me a coke; I'm going to hit the ladies room before we leave. I'll meet you at the Hobie Cat."

129

Her first encounter with Gunther stretched her imagination. The laws of physics no longer seemed to apply. She made the mistake of taking the short cut around the side of the building, instead of the long way through the dance area. Gunther grabbed her as she made the turn, he must have just arrived. She could smell the beer on his breath as he leaned into her.

She thought about running, but stood her ground. She had seen him in action, and going up against a psychopath with a god complex wasn't exactly a rational move. *Maybe I'll run.*

There really was no beginning or end to the kiss; it wasn't even really there, and because of that, it was tremendous.

Jules had never been kissed passionately before. In fact, she had never even kissed a boy before.

Any kind of enjoyment or excitement she felt quickly disappeared when he suddenly became grabby. She heard her shirt rip as he was pawing at her breasts.

Jules pushed him away, and then kicked him between the legs as hard as she could.

This time she ran.

Big John heard the commotion and turned the corner as Gunther began to rise. Jules ran right into him. He grabbed Jules by her shoulders, put her to the side, and cocked his fist.

Gunther was a nanosecond from being knocked into next week when Jules shouted to him. "Stop! I want to talk to him."

Jules walked up toward Gunther and put her foot on his chest to keep him down. "Stay there and talk, or I'll let Big John have his way."

"I didn't do anything," Gunther stammered.

"What did you do to Sandy?" Jules asked, punctuating each word. "And where is Miffy?"

"I didn't do anything to Sandy," he paused. "And who is Miffy?"

"Don't be an ass, Gunther. Mary Francis Davenport," she said. "I've heard enough BS." She turned toward Big John. "Grab him, he's coming with us, and he's going to talk."

GENE HILGREEN

15

Anna's Island
Friday Night April 5th

Jack and Emma were at the Tiki bar with a few of the tight knit Corporation members when Jules pulled up to Anna's house in her golf cart.

"How was your evening?" Jack asked.

"Just great, but it's not over just yet. Jules said. She waved to the other guests before calling out, "Jack, got a second."

Jack excused himself and walked toward the golf cart. "What's the matter, honey?"

"I need your assistance at Big John's," she caught herself. "I mean Buck's house. No questions until we get there."

Jack got in the cart with Jules and hung on as she whipped it around and floored it back toward the other end of the island. When they walked in, Gunther was duct taped to a chair. Big John sat in the chair next to him using his lap as an ottoman.

Jules walked over and ripped the tape off his mouth and activated the taser on her R-CAT. "Move your feet Big John," she said, and pointed the taser at Gunther. "Start talking Gunther, or—"

"Jules," Jack interrupted. He had known Jules since she was eight, and at times had seen her act slightly psychopathic. "How about you explain what's going on here first."

Jules began her version of events, starting with the first day of school.

When Jules was finished, Jack kicked Gunther in the foot, "Your turn," he said.

Gunther started with Sunday night at the concert, and Sandy leaving with some suave guy. He described Tony's description to a T.

Jules held out the photo she had of the dark haired guy. "Was it him?"

Gunther looked at the picture, and then met Jules' eyes. "Yes. That's him."

"Continue," said Jules.

That got her a pop in the arm from Jack. "I'll handle this," he said, and pulled out his Ka-Bar—a full size US

Marine Corps fighting knife—smirking at Jules as he cut the tape that held Gunther to the chair. "Continue."

"I haven't seen Sandy since Sunday night." He looked back and forth between Jack and Jules. "Then Thursday night, Miffy and I ran into the same guy again at Louie's." He paused long enough to make Jack agitated.

"And," Jack said.

"And he said that Sandy wanted some coke, and he got it for her. Then she left him hanging." Gunther put up his hands in a surrender fashion. "We believed him, that's how Sandy rolls." Gunther paused again until he saw Jack's irritation being telegraphed by his hands rhythmically clenching and unclenching, and he quickly added, "Listen, I don't want to get kicked out of the school, I'm not rich like Sandy and Miffy."

Jack popped his fist into his hand. "Start talking, Gunther."

"Okay. Okay. He offered to turn Miffy and me on. We accepted. When we got to his van he laid out a couple of lines. I passed out almost immediately. When I woke up I was in the dunes just north of Andy Bowie Park."

"Where was Miffy?" Jules asked.

"Jules," said Jack in warning. His eyes were dead serious.

"Sorry."

Jack's icy stare returned to Gunther. "Continue."

"Miffy wasn't there. I started walking back to Louie's to get my car when I came to Blackbeard's Tavern. I stopped in for a couple of beers and shots—".

"What's your excuse for tonight," said Jules. "You tried to rape me at Louie's . . . you were drunk."

Gunther lowered his eyes as Jules approached him. "Jules . . . I'm sorry. . . . I don't know what came over me."

"You're a perv," Jules said. "That's what came over you."

Jack got between them. "I got this, Jules."

Big John rose. "Beer anyone?"

That perfect interruption made Jack laugh. "Yeah, get me one, big guy."

"Me, too," said Jules.

Jack gave Jules the *'you've got to be kidding me'* look, and then directed his gaze to everyone. "None of what we've heard leaves this room—"

"What about Anna's rules—no drugs—period," Jules said.

"I will handle Gunther," Jack said. "And you young lady . . . let the cops do their job."

Jack offered a hand to Gunther to pull him up. "Let's go," he said, and turned toward Jules. "You coming?"

She shook her head. "No. I'm staying here tonight. It's safer."

"I'm watching you, Jules," Jack said, and his finger poked his R-CAT for emphasis. "And I'm taking the cart, too."

Jules watched as the taillights of Jack's golf cart disappeared into the darkness. She put her beer down. It was untouched. She sat down next to Big John on the couch. "I heard that Greg, the spook, has a system almost as good as BADDAY."

"That he does," Big John said. "What are you thinking?"

"I'm thinking we pay him a visit tomorrow morning."

"Greg is out of town on . . . vacation."

Jules winked at Big John. "Nice cover. He's dark, too, I bet."

Big John fumbled with the key fob hanging from his belt, and found what he wanted. "But I have a key," he said, holding it up.

"Where can I sleep tonight?" Jules asked.

"Back room is all made up waiting for you."

Jules got up from the couch, and kissed Big John on the cheek. "Good. I'm beat. See you at six."

"What?"

"You heard me," Jules said. She smiled as she skipped down the hall.

Jack stopped the golf cart fifteen feet past the 'Do Not Enter' gate that Big John had erected. He motioned to Gunther to close the gate. When Gunther was out of ear shot he hit the speed dial button for Roy on his R-CAT.

137

Roy answered on the first ring. "Jack, what's the matter?"

Jack pointed at Gunther to wait. "Got a little problem over at Anna's Island"

"What? Who?"

"It's not that bad," said Jack, who knew from the GPS scan that Roy was at the lab. "I need to put a tracker in one of Jules's classmates."

"Who?"

"Roy. This is between us for now, at least until I can come up with a story for Anna."

"Fine."

"Okay. The boy's name is Gunther, and I'm bringing him to you now. I want to track his whereabouts for the next couple of days."

"Does this have anything to do with Jules?"

"Yes and no," Jack said. "I'll fill you in when we get there."

Roy watched from his corner office as Jack and Gunther drove over the bridge from Anna's island to the complex. His first thought was to call Anna. They never hid anything from each other. And if Jules were in trouble she'd want to know about it immediately. His thought about alerting Anna faded as quickly as it had come. Jack was one of the inner core members of the Corporation, and he loved Jules, too. Besides, Anna had enough on her plate right now with Buck and Char. He had the tracker gun ready when Jack and Gunther walked into his office.

"Have a seat," Roy said. Gunther sat and Jack stood behind him.

Jack noted the two large monitors on the wall had the photos Jules and BADDAY had collected. He also noticed one of the monitors on Roy's desk showed three blinking Avatars. One was Emma at Anna's house. The other two were Jules and Big John at the other beach house. "So you're aware of Jules' little escapade."

"Yes. Anna is aware, too, to a point," Roy paused, then he added, "She asked me to keep a close eye on her."

"Well, Jules has been told to back off," said Jack.

Roy laughed. "Come on Jack. You of all people should know that Jules doesn't take orders kindly."

Jack began laughing, as well. "I know, but I told her anyway. I'm keeping a close eye on her, too."

Roy walked around his desk and stood next to Gunther. "Give me your right arm."

Gunther complied and took the shot without batting an eye.

Roy motioned up at the monitor that had the three blinking Avatars. He pressed a key on his R-CAT, and the monitor zoomed out to show blinking Avatars across all of South Padre Island. "See the three Avatars right there," he said, pointing a laser pen at them. "That green one right there is you."

"How long do I have to wear the tracker?" Gunther asked.

"Until we decide what to do with you," Jack said.

"Am I getting kicked out of the program?"

"That is up to you, Gunther," Jack said. "You stay clean and out of trouble, and I'll discuss it with Roy and Anna. As I see it, you were set up."

"Thank you," Gunther said. "I will help any way I can."

Jack walked over to the large monitor showing photos on it and saw that Gunther was in several of them. He turned toward Roy. "Can you explain to this dumb Marine what this array of pictures represents?"

Roy explained the facial recognition program process that BADDAY used to identify multiple occurrences of people in those photos or video feeds throughout the island that had Sandy Russell and, or Mary Francis Davenport in them.

"Gunther," said Jack. "Come here and tell me if you recognize any of these other people."

Roy created a folder on BADDAY with the people Gunther identified. Only two of the people identified were not students, professors, or members of Jules's mother's entourage. One was Tony Labarbera, and the other was Kala Kellingworth, a socialite who was apparently on vacation hitting the hot spots.

Jack walked back toward Roy. "Listen, SPIPD is all over this, but I'm going to see Chief of Police Smith tomorrow to offer our help." Jack paused, and gave Roy his patented '*trust me*' look. "Listen . . . give me a couple of days with this before you tell Anna."

Roy smiled. He knew that Jack didn't hide secrets from Anna or Buck either. "Just keep me in the loop, Jack."

"What are you going to do with Gunther?"

Gunther looked back and forth between the two.

"I'm going to drop him off at the dorm. He's on my official probation list."

"Jack," Roy said, as he started to leave with Gunther. "BADDAY is all over this, too."

Jack nodded and left. In the hall he turned Gunther around and eyed the man menacingly. "You've heard that expression, 'Fool me once, shame on you; fool me twice—"

"I got it, Jack—"

"Make sure you do. 'Cause no one fools me twice, and lives to tell about it."

GENE HILGREEN

16

Isla Blanca Trailer Park
Saturday Morning April 6th

Tony made it back to his trailer shortly after midnight, drunk as a bunghole on an old oak whiskey cask. He dropped his keys as he fumbled with the lock, not once, but twice.

"Three times the charm," he said to no one.

He stumbled in and locked the door. Turned and fell backward on the mattress fully clothed. He reached for the old pistol he kept under his pillow, wrapped his hand around the barrel, and passed out.

The nightmare snatched him so hard his body shuttered. An endless line of women shuffled past him— the last one spoke. "You killed me. You killed us all. Way too many women to ignore. Your time will come. Soon!"

Hours later he jerked up to a full sitting position, but not fully awake. He moved his feet to the floor, and put his hands on his head, trying to rub his head awake. He sat there a good while, the dream fresh in his mind. He shook his head, trying to gather his bearings. The heat in the small confines of his trailer was unbearable—he'd never turned on the AC the night before. Sweat oozed from every pore. Then suddenly, he was fully alert.

The message echoing from the police scanner sent chills through his body. A 10-57 followed by a 187— missing person and a homicide at Isla Grand Beach Resort.

Tony showered and dressed. He had to see it for himself. It couldn't have happened again.

Nice turnout.

The crowd grew as the first responders inched closer to the bandstand. Tony joined the morning rush of sun worshippers who flocked to the beach at Isla Grand Beach Resort to claim their turf. Today they just gawked.

Mary Frances "Miffy" Davenport's body was propped up on the stage as nude as the day she was born—dead, with two Xs gouged into her. One slashed across her chest, the other her forehead.

A hand tapped him on the shoulder. "Did you know the girl?" asked a female voice behind him.

Tony froze. The beach was filling up with reporters, and he did not want his face on the news.

He pulled his cap down and turned slowly toward the voice. *Definitely not a reporter. Reporters don't wear hot pink bikini's that barely cover their assets.*

She stood five-eight, with a perfectly toned body, and a deep Southern Texas tan. Her lush chocolate-brown hair with blonde undertones was twisted up in a bun that looked like it would fall free with one shake of her head. Long diamond earrings hung from each of her lobes—cuddling a face that demanded to be looked at. However, Tony's eyes fell to her ample cleavage.

"I'm sorry," Tony said. "Were you talking to me?" His ogling put on hold as he locked eyes with her. *Dark brown, like bullet holes,* he thought. *If they are the gateway to her soul, I'd better duck when she blinks—*

"Only if you feel like talking," she said. "I'm Kala Kellingworth."

The girl was as rich as her name, Tony thought. "Sorry. I don't speak American Express."

Kala beamed, and a sexy laugh left her hot pink lips. She eyed Tony up and down. "No problem, I have my daddy's black card."

Tony's eyes lit up. "Did I say my name was Tony?"

"That's some handiwork," she said, and pointed at Miffy's sliced up body.

Tony took one more look back at the propped up girl, and then back at Kala. "I would sure like to meet whoever did this—"

You just got your wish, she thought, and smiled. *The idiot doesn't even recognize me.* She pulled out a business card with the name Kala Kellingworth—Entrepreneur, and handed it to Tony. "Call me."

Tony took the card. "Well, Kala . . . I have to run, but I'll give you a call."

She slowly parted her sexy lips and smile. "Don't wait too long, Tony. I'm only here another week."

Tony couldn't get away from the scene fast enough. "Tonight. . . Louie's Backyard," he said, and turned to leave.

"It's a date, Tony."

Tony briefly turned his head back toward the rich stunner. He nodded and smiled, but his face displayed frustration and confusion.

The killer watched as Tony picked up his pace, and smiled. "Yes Tony," she whispered. "Someone is messing with you, but you're too stupid to figure it out."

Sweat poured down Tony's cheeks as he fumbled with the keys to his trailer. He started thinking about all the murders he'd got away with already. He was doing just fine on South Padre Island until this. Someone from his past was determined to right justice. Once inside his trailer, he looked around at the mess, and his eyes finally settled on the cash, credit cards, and jewelry on the kitchen table.

Time to get out of here, he thought. *But I'm not leaving until I have the bitch in the red Ferrari.*

Under his bed he kept a couple of duffle bags. He loaded the stash in one, and his clothes in another.

He picked up the pair of cell phones that belonged to the dead girls and thought of throwing them out. *Nah. I'll sell 'em.* He chucked them in with the cash.

Tony liked the trailer because it was convenient for getting to work and for hitting the clubs, but someone was watching him. He was sure of that.

Just over the bridge—state-side Texas—sat Port Isabel. It might as well have been Mexico, but it had cheap lodging for the immigrants who maintained the hotels on the island. Tony knew the places were dives, but the residents were discrete.

He locked up the trailer, tied the bags onto his motorcycle, and then headed for Port Isabel.

Tony took a left at the only traffic light in town, and headed south for hotel row—a series of rundown, cash up front, don't-ask, don't-tell living quarters. Women of the night were advertising their assets in front of each hostel. A girl that couldn't be a day over ten approached him as he pulled his bike up to the last building.

"*Mestah*—" she managed to say before Tony cut her off.

"Beat it, kid," he said, and fished in his pocket for a couple of dollars. Kala Kellingworth's business card fell to the ground.

The girl bent down to pick up the card.

"Give me that," he said. "Here's two dollars—now beat it." The girl handed the card to Tony, snatched the bills, and ran. Tony looked at the card and smiled. *That woman was hot, but something about her rubbed me wrong. She did say she'd be in town for a week. I'll have to think about it.* He tucked the card back in his money clip and entered the hostel.

He paid the manager upfront a hundred bucks for the next week and checked out the prostitutes seated around the room. A young woman with dyed blonde hair—her dark roots were already showing—grabbed his fancy. She reminded him of the rich Ferrari chick. A lecherous smile spread across his face. He pointed at her. "You'll do," he said. "Follow me." The young woman stood, and then followed Tony to his room.

17

Greg's Beach House
Saturday Morning April 6th

Jules had Big John up, ready, and out the door by six-thirty. Jules captained the Hobbie Cat south, and twenty minutes later steered into one of three dock spaces rented by the Corporation at South Padre Island Fishing. Greg always kept a red, white, and blue dune buggy parked at the slip.

"I'm driving," said Big John.

That got him *the look* from Jules who held out her hand for the keys. "Thanks Big guy," she said. "Where to?"

"Make a left on East Palmetto," he said. "Take it to the end . . . can't miss it."

Greg Correa's two story beach house stood majestically on Gulf Boulevard between East Sunset drive and East Palmetto Drive. Jules pulled up to the three car garage.

Big John hopped out of the buggy and headed to the gate separating the front from the back. "This way," he said, and a grin spread across his face. "Front door is a façade."

"Wow, Big John," Jules said. "Using big words, are we?"

Big John smiled and continued to the deck in the back yard.

"Wow again," said Jules. A set of waves crashed on the shoreline laying just over one-hundred feet from the back deck. She admired the perfectly landscape yard and the copse of palm trees that populated the adjacent lots.

"He owns the lots on both sides," Big John said. "Likes his privacy."

"We can hang out later," said Jules. "Let's see the equipment first."

"He'll be home this afternoon. Maybe you should call him first . . . before you touch anything."

Jules smirked, but decided she would be pissed if someone messed with her stuff. "Fine," she said. "Hell, he probably has it booby trapped, anyway."

Greg answered on the third ring. "So, Jules, how do you like my yard."

"How do you know—"

"Cameras picked you up as soon as you passed through the gate," Greg interrupted. "I'm a retired spook. What did you expect?"

"So listen. . . I'd like to get access to your system."

"What's wrong with BADDAY?"

Jules paused. "I don't want Anna, Roy, or Jack knowing I'm snooping around."

Greg laughed. "You'll make a fine spook someday," he said. "Okay, user ID is j-u-l-1-3-t-a-1-7; password is Jules—uppercase J—lowercase u-l-e-s. You will have to change it."

"Thanks Greg."

"Happy birthday, Jules, I will be there a little after twelve," he said. "Hey, put the big guy on."

Jules handed the phone to Big John. "He wants to talk to you."

Big John took the phone. "Sup?"

"Listen, I'm not, too thrilled about this," Greg said. "You just watch her ass, and I want a full explanation later."

"I got her."

"Later." Greg hung up.

"Okay, Jules, follow me," Big John said, as he opened the back door.

After an hour and forty minutes of testing the system, Jules was convinced that Greg's system had all the tracking programs that BADDAY had. While running her pictures and videos through Greg's facial recognition system, she poked around for hidden directories and files.

It was almost noon when she found a well hidden CIA folder. Greg had access to the new CIA satellite, and she wasn't surprised it had access to thousands of satellites giving the CIA 24/7 coverage of SPI.

Jules looked toward Big John who was creating a pyramid with his empty Tecate cans. "Seems like Uncle Snowdan is afraid he might miss something that happens at the research center."

"Hey, I just do what they tell me," Big John said, and cracked open another can. "Greg should be here soon, so you ought to hurry up."

Jules thought about several conversations she had with Grandpa Buck. *DCI Snowdan Jones is my friend, but he is still the head of the CIA. Take what he says with a grain of salt, and be careful what you say to him. He always has his own agenda.*

"The CIA is spying on the research center," Jules said to empty ears.

Big John put his hands up in surrender. "Greg doesn't tell me everything . . . just who to hit."

Jules downloaded the satellite access program to her R-CAT, and was logging off the system when Greg walked into the command center.

"Find what you wanted?" Greg said.

Jules knew she was caught. "Yes," she said. "Tell Uncle Snowdan thanks."

"What, and get shot? Consider it one of your birthday gifts."

"How good is that new satellite?"

Greg winked. "What satellite?"

Big John stood. "Beer anyone?"

"Corona with fruit," Greg said. "How about you Jules?"

"Waters, fine," she said. "Thanks, Big John."

Greg pulled up a chair next to Jules. "How about filling me in on your little project," he said. "Maybe I can help out."

Jules went back to her first day of class, and told him everything.

"How far back do the tapes go on the new satellite?"

"It's been up for twenty days," he said. "But the CIA is still testing."

Big John came back with a Corona, a bottle of water, and two Tecates for himself. He handed Greg and Jules their drinks, and then turned on the TV. A local reporter who Big John knew well was at the Isla Grand Beach Resort standing inches from a roped off area near the band stage.

Jules looked up when she heard the word *Davenport* loud and clear. "Big John, make that louder," she said.

Across the bottom of the screen scrawled, "Mary Francis Davenport found dead at Isla Grand Beach Resort . . . investigation underway."

Jules, Greg, and Big John left Greg's house for the Isla Grand Beach Resort. They were confronted immediately by SPIPD Chief of Police Jerry 'Smitty' Smith. Chief Smith had known Greg and Big John for over twenty years, and even moonlighted by protecting Greg's place when the man was out of town.

"Greg," he said, rather abruptly twisting his handlebar mustache. "What's your interest in this?"

A tad shorter than Greg, Chief Smith removed his hat, and offered a hand. The sun was reflecting off Smitty's bald head, blinding Greg. "Smitty," he said, rather pleasantly while opening his arms for a hug. "Tell me how you really feel."

"Listen, this is a local matter, and I don't want the CIA or FBI nosing in on it," he said, relaxing his tone a tad. "This is my island."

"Come on Smitty, we're just here to help."

"Who's the young lady?"

Jules stuck out her hand as Greg introduced her. "Meet Buck Davidssen's granddaughter, Jules."

"I've known your grandpa a long time, too," he said. "So what's going on, Greg?"

"Why don't we go back to my place and talk," Greg said. "Jules can fill you in. . . she's becoming quite the sleuth."

Almost an hour had passed, and Chief Smith had seen and heard enough. "Listen, young lady, I appreciate everything you have done for us, but—"

"Chief Smith, I can help."

Smitty let out a big Texas laugh. He looked straight into Jules' eyes and then at Greg. "Wonder where she gets that from."

Big John put his hands up in surrender.

"I can help," Jules repeated.

"You helped enough," Chief Smith said. "There have been two murders that we know about." He paused; almost waiting for Jules to interrupt him again, but she just stared at the floor. "I don't want you snooping around anymore."

Jules reached around her back to make sure the Glock was covered.

The movement did not go unnoticed. "And I'll pull that gun permit if I hear anything," Chief Smith said. "This is a local matter, and you're twenty pounds of TNT in a five pound bag waiting to explode."

"I've been called worse," she said.

"Watch it! Or I'll pull your gun permit right now." He looked at Greg and Big John. "I'm holding you two responsible to reel her in—if you get my meaning."

Greg and Big John nodded.

After a few more minutes of conversation, Jules convinced Chief Smith she was off the case.

155

Greg's phone rang, the caller ID displayed DCI Jones. "I gotta take this," he said and walked into another room. "Yo."

"Greg, this is no laughing matter," said DCI Snowdan Jones.

"Sorry, boss—won't happen again."

"DDHS Livingston and I were called back to DC," he said. "Something big is brewing. I understand that Chief Smith and SPIPD have your current problem under control?"

"Yes," Greg said. He believes it's a local matter, and wants to keep it that way."

"Fine then. Keep me informed—out."

Greg put his R-CAT back in his pocket, and walked back into the other room. "DCI and DDHS are headed back to DC."

"Good," said Chief Smith. "I'm going to send a crew out to pick up Labarbera for questioning." He winked at Jules as he said it. "Remember, I'm watching you, Jules." He pointed two fingers at his eyes for emphasis, and then left.

18

Anna's Island
Saturday Night - Jules' Birthday Party

Flames of yellow, orange, and red effervesced from the teepee of mesquite, cherry, and black walnut logs meticulously arranged in the center of the sixteen foot round fire pit that separated the Tiki bar from the party tent. Jules smiled, taking in the mixture of burnt wood scents—knowing Big John had a hand in the construction of the fire, too.

She continued past the fire, her attention completely drawn to the LED lights that sparkled off the fractured glass of the Bamboo lights. She followed the pathway that led to the party tent. Jules closed her eyes and breathed in the cornucopia of aromas emanating from the food stations lining the perimeter of the tent—all were decked out in the finest Hawaiian luau décor. She marveled at the decorations and thought about what went into the party's appearance.

Mom and Anna went beyond all out for this party.

She spotted Big John belting out orders to the servers as if he were the head chef. He made quite the spectacle, standing hands on his hips, clad in a colorful grass skirt and a chieftain Mahiole headdress, instead of his usual beat-up Popeye Doyle hat. She listened as he pointed out the finer details of cooking skirt steaks. Against the staff's better judgment, the steaks were prepared on his old, rusted, fifty-five gallon drum that had been converted into a barbeque pit—per Jules' instructions.

"Hey big guy, everything under control here?" She turned and winked at the genuine head chef who was preparing the steaks. He winked back.

"Yup . . . just making sure," replied Big John.

"Good then. Now leave the chef alone and follow me," she said. "I want you to meet someone."

Dr. Bryce Kellogg stood by the fire pit with Jules' parents, and a few other scientists from the center. When she saw Jules and Big John approaching, she left the group and walked towards them.

"Happy birthday, Jules."

"Thank you Dr. Kel—, Bryce." Jules caught herself. "I'd like you to meet my buddy Big John."

Bryce looked the mountain of a man up and down, and extended her hand. "Hello Big John, please call me Bryce."

"I'm so glad you came," Jules said.

Bryce smiled. She really liked Jules. "What to get the girl that has everything?" she said and handed Jules a small box wrapped in paper bearing tie-dyed peace signs all over it.

"Love the wrapping paper Dr. Kellogg," Jules said.

"Bryce, Jules."

"Sorry, Bryce," Jules said as she opened the box. Inside was a multi-threaded rainbow colored friendship bracelet, with a black peace sign woven into the middle.

"I made it myself. Here, let me put it on for you."

Jules hugged Bryce and kissed her cheek. "It's beautiful. Thank you."

"Good. Now scoot," said Bryce. "Go have some fun for a change. I see Jai, your lab partner, sitting all by himself over there"

"Fine."

Jules looked up at Big John and winked, jabbing him in the side with her elbow. "Ask her," she whispered in his direction, and then waved for Jai to join her. Jai jogged over, and the pair headed in the direction of the main tent.

"Um . . . Bryce . . . would you care for a drink?" Big John stammered.

"Yes, but just one. I have to keep a clear mind tonight."

She hooked her arm through Big Johns' and they headed to the Tiki bar. She hadn't planned on staying long at the party. Anna had given her a few days off so she could tend to some business at home. She had planned to leave the party by nine, but ended up staying a few minutes longer.

At nine o'clock, Jax and Ramsey stood at the center table, which was now decorated to overflowing with presents for Jules, and Ramsey called for everyone's attention. Big John pulled over a smaller table, and then placed an over-sized cake on it. The cake was designed as a gymnasium, complete with four plastic pieces of gymnastic apparatus.

Jules rushed to her mom's side, and studied the cake in closer detail. Seventeen small candles circled the large center candle, which was designed like a gymnast atop a trophy. Around the outside of the candles was printed: Happy Birthday Jules - National Vaulting Champion.

Jax lit the candles, and began to sing *Happy Birthday*. Everyone joined in.

"Make a wish, honey."

"I did, mom," she said, and blew out the candles.

"Would you like to open your presents now?" Jax asked.

Jules looked around at all the guests. "Nah, I'll open them later. Everyone is having too much fun." She looked around for Bryce, but didn't see her.

Jack and Emma approached the table, and Jack handed Jules his R-CAT. "Someone wants to speak to you," he said.

Jules took the phone. "It's Grandpa and Anna!" she yelled, while Buck and Anna sang happy birthday to her. When they were finished Jules said, "Love you both. When are you coming to the island?"

"In a couple of days," Anna said. "Both of us. Now let me speak to Jack."

Jules handed the R-CAT back to Jack, and he turned and left the tent with Emma in tow.

🔫

Gunther was not one of the students invited to Jules' birthday party, but he had fun anyway—until he saw Tony scouting out the women. He called Jack, who called Chief Smith, but by the time the SPIPD posse arrived, Tony was long gone.

After a quick search of the bar and dance floor, Tony believed Kala was messing with him and left Louie's. He wanted the girl in the red Ferrari anyway—who he recently learned was one, Jules Spenser. Feeling irritated and bored, he left for a bike ride north.

He stopped the bike on Route 100, and with his powerful binoculars, saw the lights of the party. Focusing

161

closer, he could make out a party in full swing. He panned toward the garage and saw the red Ferrari.

Damn her—

He fish-tailed the bike, and headed back to Port Isabel. He would have to settle for a hooker.

Jules decided to take her presents up to her room where she would open them later. She corralled Jai and Big John to help her. After several trips, they were piled neatly beside her bed. She then went to the door and opened it. Putting on her most pleasant smile, she said, "Okay, you two—out. I'm going to shower and change. I'll meet you at the Tiki bar later."

She watched from her doorway as they walked down the steps. Satisfied, she locked the door and accessed Sandy and Miffy's financial accounts on her R-CAT to get their credit card information, and checked their last usage. She then loaded them into the credit card APP on her R-CAT, and set the program to alert her if they were used again.

Miffed that she couldn't locate either of the girls' phones through the GPS, she tried another idea. She found Greg with Big John, Roy, and Jai at the Tiki bar. She pulled Greg aside. "Can your system run a 'find my phone' even if you don't know the carrier?"

"Jules you aren't perfect after all," he said. "You should know that *Big Brother* tracks everyone's cell."

"Thought so," she said. "Can it tell me when and where the last time either of these two numbers pinged?"

"Let me see your R-CAT for a sec."

"Why?"

"I want to see what APP's you borrowed from me."

Jules smiled and handed over the phone.

Greg found the APP he was looking for. "What's the numbers again?"

"Thanks, Master Spook," she said. "I'll take it from here."

"Hey—remember what Chief Smith said."

"Don't worry. I'll give him the locations when I locate them."

Big Brother's database was quite substantial, and it took almost twenty minutes for Jules to get the information she was looking for.

She called Chief Jerry Smith.

He answered on the fourth ring. "Hey, I'm busy here. Aren't you supposed to be having fun at your party?"

"Yeah, but—"

"What do you want?"

"It's not what I want; it's what I have for you."

"Talk."

Jules told him.

"I thought I told you to back off."

"Sorry, sir—I just wanted to help out SPIPD's finest."

163

"Jules, we gotta talk tomorrow after your parents leave."

There was laughter in his voice, thought Jules. *Maybe I'm not in trouble.* "First thing chief," she said. "I promise."

Jax and Ramsey called it a night at midnight. Jules, Jack, and Emma walked them to their car.

"Your jet will be ready at ten tomorrow," Jack said. "So meet us here for breakfast at eight, and I will chopper you to the airport after."

"Sounds like a plan," Ramsey said, and then left after kisses were exchanged.

19

Brownsville, Texas
Sunday Morning April 7th

The twenty-eight mile trip would normally take just under an hour, depending on traffic. But by helicopter it took less than fifteen minutes; the bulk of that time was spent waiting for clearance. With the airport in sight, Jules began fidgeting in anticipation. She looked over her shoulder from the co-pilot seat at her parents in the back of the Hughes. They both had earplugs in and were listening to tunes. They couldn't hear the conversation between Jules and Jack.

"Jack—"

"What?"

"Let me take her in."

Jack gave her the squinty eye. "How much time do you have in the simulator?"

"Come on—Anna lets me."

"How much?"

"Including Anna time—twenty hours"

Jack mulled it over a bit moving his lips back and forth. "How many simulator hours on landing?"

"Four."

"Liar."

"Two hours."

"Show me your log book."

Jules pulled it from her backpack and held it up for Jack to see. "Come on Jack, the outer markers are coming up, and I'm a quick learner—remember?"

Jack gave her the look again. "How do you know that?"

"Anna."

"Okay, you can take her in, but no funny stuff, and. . . rough up that squeaky voice a tad."

"Like this," Jules asked, and she emulated the deep Wolfman Jack voice from the kid in the movie, *Iron Eagle*. "This is the Blue Bird."

"Not funny Jules."

"I got it, Jack."

Jules took control of the Hughes, and addressed the control tower. "Brownsville SPI tower, this is Hughes November Too Too Sev-en Alpha Lima," she said, with a somewhat mature voice, as she gave the helicopter and tail numbers (N2275AL) in ICAO (International Civil Aviation Organization) phonics. She looked toward Jack, winked, then added. "Student pilot."

Jack nodded. "Good. Much better."

The tower responded. "Trainer November Too Too Sev-en Alpha Lima, have you in sight—stand by."

"Roger that."

"Nice job," Jack said, a few minutes later when Jules landed the Hughes MD-530-F perfectly. Her parents were none the wiser.

"Told ya," she said, and put her arm around Jack.

Jules hugged her parents as a golf cart pulled up to take them to the terminal. "Call me when you get home," she said, and watched them ride off.

"What would you like to do now?" Jack asked.

"I was thinking about hitting the gun range."

"Like the way you think," Jack said.

Jack let Jules take the bird back to Anna's island. There was a note from Emma that she was sailing with Big John and Roy, and would be back in late afternoon. Jules grabbed her favorite golf cart from the garage. She and Jack took off for the range.

The range was empty when they arrived. Jules grabbed a couple of freshly loaded magazines from the supply room while Jack unlocked the rifle vault.

"What's that?" Jules asked, watching as Jack opened an ornate rifle case and began fitting a suppressor onto its fluted barrel."

"It's an Accuracy International AX338, chambered for .338 Lapua Magnum; a gift from Char's father."

"Buck says British rifles suck."

"Not this one," Jack said. "I once took out a guy from. . ." He paused and looked up at Jules, who wore a look of amazement as if he were saying *Trey Anastasio*, the lead singer of Phish was coming to dinner. "We have a couple more in the rack chambered for .300 Winchester Magnum and 7.62x51 mm NATO rounds."

"Tell me about the shot," Jules said.

"Honey . . . you know we can't talk about our sanctions, but it was a twenty-two hundred yard shot."

Jules knew that Jack was the best sniper in Buck's old unit. She had caught parts of some old war stories when the group had too much to drink. She knew better about prying for more information, but knew that one day she would be brought into the fold. "What other goodies do you and Buck have stashed here?"

"There's a couple of AR15's, a Cheytec M200, a Weatherby Mark V TRR, and Buck's favorite: the M40A7 USMC super sniper rifle."

"I shot the Weatherby—too much kick."

"Why don't you try the AR15," Jack said. "I think you'll like the feel."

"Set me up," she said.

168

Jack pulled a forty-two inch, weather proof, rifle case from his locker and opened it. Inside the foam fitted case sat a matte black modified AR15 loaded for bear, multiple magazines, a suppressor, and two telescopic sights. He screwed on the suppressor and smacked in a loaded thirty clip magazine. "Take this for a ride," he said, handing the light-weight heart-breaker to Jules.

They shot rounds and compared targets for the next hour. Jules switched between her Glock and the AR15.

"I love this rifle, Jack."

"Thought you would. Why don't you break it down, and then we'll get some lunch before we see Chief Smith."

"You knew?"

Jack smiled. "Chief Smith called me this morning. Said to make sure your ass was there by two—his words."

Jules smile back. "His words," she said, emphasizing it with air quotes.

"Don't worry . . . you're not in trouble . . . he just wants to pick your mind."

Jules' grin spread from ear to ear. When she was done breaking down the AR15, she closed the case. Etched in sparkling gold letters on the top of the case was the following: *Property of Jules Spenser.*

"Jack?"

"Happy birthday, honey."

Jack looked at his watch as they were passing the flight simulator room—it was a quarter past noon. "Hold up a sec, Jules."

She stopped in her tracks and followed him into the room. No one was in the Hughes simulator.

"Get in," he said. "I want to see how you handle a couple of distractions."

Jack threw everything in the book at Jules for the next half hour—rain, sleet, snow, and gale force winds to name but a few. Jules landed safely each time. "Is that all you got, Jack?" she said over the com."

"Well. . . I could give you an engine failure. You're going to have to learn it anyway to get your license."

"Do it."

Jules had read up on autorotation of the main rotor blades just out of curiosity, but she had never practiced it. She knew there was different glide angles based on the weather conditions. She also knew if she didn't remain cool, calm, and act immediately—the bird would drop from the sky like a rock. But in all cases a correct glide angle had the effect of producing an upward flow of air that would spin the main rotor at some optimal RPM, storing kinetic energy in the blades.

As the helicopter approached the ground, she knew she had to get rid of most of the forward motion and slow the descent using the stored up kinetic energy in the rotors. If done right, the landing would be quite gentle. *So they say*, she thought.

Jack started with perfect weather conditions, and then moved on to rain and snow. Jules landed good enough to pass on the first two, but was a tad rough on the last one.

"Okay, Jules, here comes the wind. Remember to flare it."

The helicopter started to spin out of control. Her glide angle was way off, and when she executed the flare by pitching the nose up, the tail of the helicopter smashed into the ground, and *Failed* flashed on the screen. Jules got out of the simulator. "Well that's going to need some work," she said.

"You did good, for you first time. Now you know what you have to practice on."

"Yeah. Can we get some lunch before we see the Chief—I skipped breakfast and I'm starving."

🔫

Thick smoke drifted from Chief Smith's office as Jack and Jules entered. With his feet planted firmly on his desk he pointed at Jules with his fat cigar and said, "Have a seat young lady."

Jules looked toward Jack. "Thought you said—"

"Just sit," said Jack.

Chief Smith stared at Jules for a minute before speaking. "Let me see your PI license."

"What?"

"You heard me," he said. "No license—no snooping."

Jules glanced toward the floor trying to avoid eye contact with Chief Smith, but snapped to attention when he banged his desk.

"Gotcha!" Chief Smith tossed a deputy badge onto the desk. "I'm using the 'Posse Comitatus Act', and deputizing you as an advisor—for this investigation only."

"I'm in."

"Not so fast young lady. Sign this agreement first. And since you're a minor, Jack has agreed to sign his life away as your guardian."

"What about Anna?" Jules asked.

"This is an advisory role, Jules," Jack said. "No funny business. You're to stay out of harm's way. I'll talk to Anna when she gets back."

Jules and Jack signed the document.

"You report to me on everything, immediately." Chief Smith said. "Everything, no matter how inconsequential it may seem to you. Got it?"

"Yes, sir."

"Now tell me how you've figured this phone thing out."

For the next hour, Jules explained what she did without giving up the CIA satellite or her software. Chief Smith accepted her explanation, and said, "Fine. Maybe you can start by upgrading our software."

"I'll look at it," she said.

"Okay, now get out of here.

I got an investigation that requires my attention."

Jules tucked her badge in her pocket as she and Jack left the office.

"What do you want to do now? Jack asked.

"I want to go home, play back the events of the past few days, and come up with a plan."

GENE HILGREEN

20

Seabreeze III Resort
Sunday April 7th

Dr. Bryce Kellogg had a knack for programming—one might go so far as to call her a serious hacker. She accessed all of the accounts of the two men she hated most—Dr. Russell and Dr. Davenport. Her other hobby was surveillance systems. Sandy Russell and Mary Francis Davenport made it very easy for Bryce to keep up-to-date on their family events the girls' habit of trying to one-up each other and then posting their victories on social media.

When Sandy and Mary Francis were accepted at the South Padre Island School for Advance Nanoscience Research, Bryce did everything she could to get hired. She offered to work for free. Dr. Anna Semyonova was impressed with her background and offered her a grant instead.

Bryce began to formulate her plan for revenge, and it was a stroke of good fortune to have Tony Labarbera walk right into her plans. It was child's play setting him up to become the patsy. The idiot's own actions couldn't have fit better into Bryce's plans.

A hippie at heart, Bryce chose her outfits that she wore to the research center carefully, but under her disguise, baggy clothes and granny glasses, was a woman with a killer body—just as beautiful as Dr. Anna Semyonova and Kala Kellingworth.

Bryce was well aware of the capabilities of the system they called BADDAY. She quickly picked up on Dr. Roy Singh's affection for her and played on it. This awarded her one-on-one time in the labs with him. That time was spent learning about all the surveillance systems BADDAY had to offer. She had already studied the finer points of beating facial recognition systems well before she applied to the school. Furthermore, with her studies in Quantum Electrodynamics and Electromagnetic Radiation, Bryce was very familiar with Faraday's Law predicting how a magnetic field would interact with an electric circuit to produce an electromotive force (EMF)—a phenomenon called electromagnetic induction. She also knew that the entire research center had a sophisticated Faraday Shield that blocked external static and non-static electrical fields. Besides its security aspect, it also protected the electronic equipment from lightning and electrostatic discharges.

Although EMP (Electro Magnetic Pulse) weapons were globally outlawed, that did not stop terrorists and *wannabes* from building them. EMP's with a simple modification of radar could bounce pulses of energy off of aircraft, vehicles, and other objects—frying their electronics as the wave moves outward. Non-nuclear EMP weapons had the potential to devastate the electronic systems of areas as large as a city or as small as a selected object, without being seen, heard, or felt by anyone.

The governing body of the South Padre Island Advance Nanoscience Research Center—all core members of The Corporation—believed that an EMP at the nano level would have many medical, and other worldly uses. Anna had assigned Bryce to her pet project, where the scientists would engineer nanobots for medical procedures. Bryce jumped at the opportunity, and built a few programmable nanobots sans the protective ferrous nanoparticle field—a fail-safe—that would allow a nano EMP or MRI to deactivate the device by shorting out the circuitry in case of a failure.

🔫

With Kala Kellingworth off skiing in Argentina for the next several weeks, Bryce took the opportunity to work on her disguise. Kala had several wigs, and a wardrobe befitting her rich lifestyle.

Her transformation to the beautiful Kala was easy.

Bryce had lied to Kala about her tough schedule—she could sleepwalk through the classes she had to teach. Her research was a calling—not a chore, and she spent most of her time in the labs perfecting her plans for revenge.

Kala and Bryce were the same height and weight. They even wore the same bra size, although Bryce preferred to go natural most of the time. She enjoyed dressing up as Kala, and even got a kick out of the frilly, lace bras.

None of the students recognized her when she hit the hot spots at night as Kala—not even Jules, but Bryce made sure to keep her distance. She was approached by men of all social backgrounds, but mainly by horny frat boys looking to add another notch to their belt. She stopped them dead in their tracks with a coy 'you're not my type'. When they inquired who *was,* she simply pointed out the hottest girls near her. That sent them packing fast enough.

Dr. Bryce Kellogg chose Tony Labarbera her third week at the SPI Advanced Nanoscience Research Center. With an IQ lower than the 72 degrees the HVAC was set for, he was saddled with the moniker 'Room Temperature Tony', by the staff that had the misfortune of dealing with him.

Bryce, on the other hand, had an IQ of 150—she would play him like a puppet. She observed how he leered at the younger shapely women who worked and interned at the research center. The man was definitely a pig and a pervert.

Tony never batted an eye at her in her Bryce persona. Transformed as the rich and beautiful Kala, she caught his attention, but he didn't make a move. Surprised by his inaction, she dug deeply into his past with the help of BADDAY and uncovered his modus operandi. She knew he preyed on the rich, and was a murderer. Bryce reasoned that Tony shied from her because he was afraid of beautiful and powerful women. She knew he was after money and sex, but more than that, Tony liked young girls. He would pay dearly for that mistake.

She never wore lipstick but did wear false teeth while parading around as Bryce. That changed the configuration of her mouth. She also installed special plugs in her nose that flattened her perfect slope just enough.

At night when she was on the prowl, she chose to always wear oversized Gucci sunglasses. Just wearing a wig would not fool a facial recognition system—it was how you wore it that did. One of her eyes was always covered, and her lips were redefined with the wonders of lipstick and liners.

The oversized sunglasses she wore would beat ninety-five percent of the facial recognition algorithms used by security systems. By styling the wigs so that it covered one of her eyes—she would beat ninety-nine percent of the systems. She hoped it included BADDAY, but there were always other factors to consider.

Jules Spenser with her genius IQ and eidetic mind was one of those factors that haunted Bryce.

A Phish Pheak herself, Bryce attended Phish's concerts every night, dressed in her wildest hippie attire. She followed Sandy and Mary Francis who were dressed for action. It didn't take long for Tony to zero in on them. Hell, Bryce could see the jewelry flashing fifty feet away.

Under her lightweight long sleeve top and ankle length granny dress, Bryce wore a black compression body suit that kept her cool and let her skin breathe. When she followed Tony to his hide-out, she was out of the dress in seconds. Her wig and designer military-grade night vision sunglasses completed her ensemble.

She tailed Tony for weeks and noted how he plied his victims with drugs when the opportunity availed itself. Sandy was not the first victim who fell for Tony's offer of uncut drugs. She had watched with amusement when Tony choked Sandy during his perverted sex act.

Do my job for me, Tony, she thought, but she was later disappointed.

With Mary Francis, he used the same MO, but there was a third party—Gunther—the tall extremely handsome classmate. Bryce was impressed with how the bungling

Tony drugged and rid himself of Gunther's intrusion, before he had his way with Mary Francis.

Both times, he had left the girls without a care in the world. When she found the two girls, they were very much alive, although heavily drugged.

She finished Tony's job on Sandy by strangling her, but Mary Francis—Miffy—would become a statement to the world.

Disappointment exuded from Bryce's face when she first uncovered Miffy. Certain that she was dead, Bryce had begun to bag her. But doing a cursory check, she felt the barest pulse at the nape of Miffy's neck. The girl was heavily drugged and might have eventually OD'd if left alone.

Knowing Tony's MO, she stocked her 'go' bag with a syringe of pure opioid antagonist, and titrates to reverse respiratory depression. She revived Miffy to the point of cognizance and locked eyes with her. With one hand around her throat, she carved a deep X into her chest and forehead, and then planted the stiletto to the hilt through the one on her forehead.

She kept the girls bodies on ice, in a deep freezer, on a boat that she picked up for cheap, and later docked at the South Padre Island Fishing docks.

Her disguise was perfect and no one recognized her when she followed Tony on a nightly basis, she also learned that Jules liked to take out the red Ferrari and run the gears. An early riser and lover of speed herself, Bryce followed Jules several times on her modified Loncin

181

LX650 crotch-rocket motorcycle. Her top speed of 136 mph couldn't compare with the Ferrari, but she got to see Jules swim out to the sandbar with the red and white flag.

Jules' eidetic and computer-like mind concerned Bryce. She liked Jules, but no one was going to get in the way of her revenge.

She decided to see what Jules was made of and shake her up a bit with Sandy's body by staging it on the sandbar. But when she staged Miffy's body, it was to shake up Tony. As a kicker, she left enough evidence that Tony would take the rap.

The night that Tony was expecting to meet Kala, Bryce left a nano device in Miffy and Sandy's bags that was sure to accompany the bodies' home. Then she hid the girls' clothing, which Tony had left at his trailer, where she believed only the cops would find them. That done, she returned to Kala's penthouse suite and planned her revenge for Dr. Russell and Dr. Davenport, who were sure to come and identify their daughters.

One way or another, she would bring down their private aircraft. When and where would be determined soon. Bryce had learned at Jules' party that Russell and Davenport were flying a Gulfstream G550 into Brennan Farm Airport early next week.

Bob Brennan was a close friend of the two doctors, and his farm was located four miles south of Los Fresnos and Highway 100, which is the gateway to SPI, and mainly used by crop dusters who rented hanger space. She also learned they would chopper into Anna's island after they landed.

She knew from experience that it would be a VFR (Visual Flight Rules) flight, and the tower would be manned. But the pilot would receive multiple IFR (Instrument Flight Rules) from neighboring airports—including Brownsville/South Padre Island International airport when it reached their outer markers. She would pay a visit as the rich and sexy Kala Kellingworth looking for hanger space and hack Brennan's communication, barometric, and instrument landing systems, just in case.

GENE HILGREEN

21

**SPI Advanced Nanoscience Research Center
Monday April 8th**

The ping from the clock was the only thing that emanated from the kitchen as Jules made her way down the stairs and popped her head in for a look. The LED wall clock flashed 6:01. Absent from the room was the sweet smell of Russian blend and Anna.

Jules expected to see Jack up, and realized better when she peeked out a couple of windows. She spotted the four guards in a coordinated patrolling pattern. Dressed in camouflage BDU T-shirts and trousers with The Corporations snake-eater logo on the chest—these guards were hard core Marines who passed Gunny's snake-eater program.

Jack felt safe, she thought. *He was probably still in bed sleeping with Emma.* She smiled, and then said aloud for her own benefit, "Fat chance that Emma would be up this early."

When she walked out the front door on to the deck, she pointed her R-CAT at the garage for effect and pressed the icon. The garage doors opened.

The Ferrari looked enticing, and made her think of Anna. *Later* she though, and chose a golf cart instead. She raced over the bridge, and dropped the cart off with maintenance. She passed through security without a hitch, and aimed straight for the gun range.

The gun range was empty, and Jules alternated between the Glock and her AR-15—shooting a couple of magazines each. She cleaned up her area, and packed her assault weapon back in her locker. Before leaving, she tucked the Glock safely in a holster attached to her back and felt relaxed and secure by the feel of its weight.. As she passed the flight simulator room she took a peek and saw it was empty. *Later for that, Roy will be in by now,* she thought, and took off for the data center, stopping for two large coffees on the way.

🔫

The door to Roy's office was open, and Jules knocked. A voice that sounded like Anna said, "Good morning Jules, you may enter."

"Ha ha to you, too, BADDAY. Where is Dr. Singh?"

"He's in the ba—"

"That will be all, BADDAY," Roy said, as he exited his private bathroom. "Jules, what can I do for you?"

Jules flashed her deputy badge, and placed the double latte mocha on Roy's desk.

"Thank you, Jules, I needed that." He smiled, took a sip, and then added. "I heard from Jack that Chief Smith has asked for your programming services." He looked Jules dead on—no smile this time. "Not for your sleuthing services."

"Yeah, yeah. I got the fourth degree from Jack already."

"So. . ."

"I found some pretty interesting stuff on Greg's computer," she said. "Do you know the CIA is spying on us?"

Roy laughed. "Remember what your grandfather said about the CIA."

Now it was Jules turn to laugh. "Keep your friends close, and your enemies closer."

"Good," Roy said. "You're learning."

"He said to trust Uncle Snowdan as far as I can throw him."

"Better." Roy took another sip, and then sat behind his desk. "We know about the new satellite the CIA launched," Roy said. "But I haven't hacked in yet for the codes. Greg told me at your party that it's not working yet"

Jules pulled a 128GB memory flash drive from her pocket and handed it to Roy. "There are some pretty interesting programs on that drive. I found them in a hidden folder on Greg's network. You might want to take a look."

"I figured your curiosity would somehow lead to you finding a way into Greg's computer," Roy said, and laughed. "That's why I didn't hack in. I was going to ask you about it at lab today."

"Oh, about that. I was going to skip lab. But if you like we can discuss it now."

"Have a seat."

Roy loaded the drive into a test environment on BADDAY. "Nothing goes into production without Buck, Anna, and my signoff," he said. "I'll spend more time with this later. I have a lecture at eight to prepare for, and you should be getting to your lab class."

Jules got up and started to leave.

"Jules." When she turned back toward him, he continued, "Thanks. You've saved me a ton of time."

"Anytime, Dr. Singh," she said, and proudly pranced out of the office.

Damn, Roy thought. *She's got Buck written all over her.*

Jai looked up from his workstation when Jules entered the lab. He gained her attention when she sat down by pointing at his watch. "You're late."

She logged onto the system, and then turned toward him with a large smile. "I was with Uncle Roy, working." She gave Jai as close to a flirting sneer as she could. "Besides, we have a substitute today . . . remember?"

Jules's eyes lit up when Dr. Lyn Alexander walked into the classroom. Her gleam was not from surprise—it was pure admiration. She had researched all the scientists at the facility. Dr. Alexander had an interesting history: Fifteen years in the Royal Canadian Air Force before she became a veterinarian. She specialized in animal behavior, and now was a leader in nanobiotechnology for animal, medical diagnostics.

Jules turned toward Jai, and whispered, "She's working in the robotics lab with Emma."

"If I may have your attention . . . I am Dr. Lyn Alexander, and I will be covering for Dr. Kellogg for the next couple of days. She has left a detailed schedule for this class." Dr. Alexander looked about the classroom and saw inquiring faces. "Any questions before we begin."

A girl, younger than Jules, raised her hand. *How cute*, thought Jules.

Dr. Alexander looked at the name tag on the workstation. "Yes, Donna Esna. Go ahead."

"Dr. Alexander, can you tell us anything about the robotics project you're working on."

189

"Please call me Lyn, and I'd prefer not to talk about it here," Dr. Alexander said. "But you're more than welcome to visit the lab in your free time."

No more hands went up, and the lecture began.

At the first break, a couple of students, including Donna, accosted Dr. Alexander, and pushed about the robotics project again. She relented, and gave a perfected summary speech that gave just enough information to satisfy the inquiring minds. At five to one she ended the lecture.

"What are you doing for lunch, Jules?" Jai asked.

She had expected this question and was ready for it. "I have a one on one with Emma. I'll catch up with you later."

Jai bought the lie, and Jules left. Her golf cart was waiting for her in space number five, and then she raced over the bridge for Anna's house.

Jules counted four guards as she pulled into the garage. Knowing Jack, there were at least two more snipers out there somewhere expertly hidden. She hit the icon for the front door and entered. The distinct sound of broadcast news echoed out from the den. Jules found Jack with a sniper rifle—field stripped—on the coffee table in front of him. With a magnetic flashlight attached at one end, he was eyeing the inside of the barrel from the other—an assortment of solvents and fine cloth rags rested in arms reach.

Jack looked up as Jules entered, and went back to work. "There're sandwiches in the frig, if you hungry."

"Who made them?"

"What if I said I did? Would you starve yourself?"

"No. . . I trust you," Jules said, laughing.

"Anna made them. She didn't want her little baby to suffer."

Jules grabbed a sandwich and sat next to Jack. "What is that? Looks brand new."

"M40A7 Marine sniper rifle, and it is. Got it this morning, straight from the factory. I'm testing it for the Corps."

"What's the range?"

Jack looked toward Jules. "With the new scope and base, it's got a 200 MOA (Minute of Arc). I'd say twenty-eight-hundred yards with some fine adjustments." Jack held the scope to his eye and played with the knob. "The good thing is that it takes almost six seconds to travel that far. So I pop one off, raise it an RCH higher, and then pop off another."

"What's an RCH?"

"Real small." Jack said, and held out his index finger with his thumb under it about a quarter inch apart. He placed them in front of one eye and squinted."

"Oh, I get it. Royal—that's not funny, Jack."

"Sorry," Jack said, and added a teasing smile. "Now get out of here. I'm busy."

GENE HILGREEN

22

Padre Boulevard - Route 100
Monday afternoon April 8th

Jules stuffed the remainder of her sandwich into her mouth, and grabbed another from the fridge before she left the house for the garage. She plugged in her R-CAT, and started the Ferrari.

"Find Big John," she said, and the GPS program zoomed in on the other end of Anna's island. She saw Big John sunning himself on his Hobbie Cat a Corona in his hand. Jules sent him a text message. "Taking a run. Try not to spill your beer. C U in half an hour." Jules watched the screen as Big John spilt his beer on his chest reaching for his phone. She laughed and then eased the Ferrari out.

She shifted from first to second without hitting the gas so the car would purr and not roar. Jules made a right onto Route 100 and drove south past Andy Bowie Park to the next turnaround. She made a U-turn and then gunned the beast. Her goal was to break Anna's record—two-hundred-twenty-two MPH had a nice ring to it.

The SPIPD officer sitting in his car having lunch at Clayton's Beach Bar never saw Jules make the turn at the Andy Bowie Park turnaround. Smitty put his beer and burger down when his radar registered the motorcycle that blew past him at sixty-five MPH in a thirty MPH zone. He gave chase with his siren blasting and pulled Tony Labarbera over just past Edwin King Atwood Park.

"What's your hurry, son," Smitty asked.

"Sorry, Sir," Tony said. "I'm late for work."

"That's no excuse for driving double the limit," the officer said, his hand resting on his gun. "Off the bike. License and registration."

Tony handed them over, and his badge for the South Padre Island Advance Nanoscience Research Center fell to the ground.

Smitty motioned for Tony to pick it up. Tony handed the badge over, too. A smile spread across his face when he read the badge. "So . . . you work for Dr. Semyonova?"

Tony saw a chance to pour on his charm. He had several outstanding warrants, and knew he would get arrested if the officer called in his name. "Yes, sir. I take care of her office and laboratory."

Smitty raised his sunglasses, and his smile turned into a mischievous grin. "Tell Anna that Chief Smith said howdy." He gave the license and registration back to Tony. "Consider this a warning—watch the speed limit."

"Thank you, sir." Tony got back on his bike and maintained the speed limit until he passed the research center, then he opened it up. The office might have missed Jules, but Tony didn't.

Tony's day hadn't gone as easy as he had hoped. His boss gave him a beat down at the supply building regarding complaints from staff at the center. Tony had broken his only rule: No flirting or contact with the client. Tony didn't stop with just flirting. His lascivious behavior included groping and vulgar remarks to female employees and students. Tony was fired on the spot.

He left the building and headed home to his trailer in silence. He was replaying in his mind about the girls he had groped, when a red Ferrari blew past him going the other way.

There was another turnaround just north of the park and Jules took it. She continued south to the turnaround of her original start point. She expected normal traffic with spring break over, and would make the best of it. No excuses. She'd let the big dog eat.

She blew by Edwin King Atwood Park, and two seconds later the Ferrari chirped two-hundred-fifty kilometers-per-hour. The next Russian accented warble of three-hundred kilometers per hour came at the sign to the entrance of the SPI Advanced Nanoscience Research Center. Jules knew that she had four miles of real estate left before the road ended.

The Ferrari came standard with carbon-ceramic brakes, which delivered immense and assured stopping power. But nothing about this car was standard. Jules was confident she could stop the car in less than 2500 feet at 220 MPH. She had broken the barrier twice—with Buck holding on for dear life on the open roads outside of Aspen. The first time was in Bucks million dollar Koenigsegg, Swedish hyper-car—a present from Char. The second was in Char's Lamborghini. Both cars were hot, but she liked the Ferrari better.

Island Adventure Park was looming, and the Ferrari hadn't announced three-hundred fifty yet. She had already passed the one mile to roads end marker. When a voice came over the speakers, Jules knew she was in trouble. The Ferrari would never announce four-hundred, and travelling at over three-hundred feet per second—tunnel vision had taken over.

How did Anna manage to break the two-hundred miles-per-hour barrier?

Jules had an idea. Even though the speedometer topped at three-hundred-sixty, she couldn't take her eyes off the road. She could barely move her head. The G-forces had her pinned to the headrest. "BADDAY," she screamed at the top off her voice as a cloud of sand blew across the pavement and impeded her vision. "How far to the end of Route 100—in feet?" Jules didn't want to waste a nanosecond calculating meters.

"Three-thousand feet and closing," came the voice from the speaker, and it sounded a lot like Anna yelling at her.

"Tell me when I have twenty-five-hundred feet left, or reach a speed of three-hundred-sixty kilometers per hour."

A second later, BADDAY announced, "twenty-five-hundred feet."

"Damn—"

"Three-hundred-sixty kilometers per hour. Twenty-two-hundred feet."

Jules punched her arm through the roof's opening, took her foot off from the gas pedal, and immediately began to tap the brake pedal at one second intervals.

The end of the road was coming fast, and she slammed down hard on the brake pedal. Sand swept across the road, and she began to go into a spin. She corrected the spin, but now had to spin the steering wheel back the other way.

Too late—she was spinning like a top.

GENE HILGREEN

23

Jules Island
Monday Afternoon April 8th

Jules let off the brake pedal and spun the steering wheel hard into the spin. As the car slowed from the mass of sand on what was left of the roads shoulder, she finally came to a stop. *Not bad*, she thought when she realized she was only twenty feet past the end of the road. But the Ferrari rested thirty feet from the gulf, and high tide would be coming soon.

Jules dug her Glock from out of the glove compartment and tucked it into its holster which was attached to the small of her back. Then she put on her black Vika leather jacket, grabbed her R-CAT off the passenger seat's floor, and walked toward the Gulf.

Further north, up the beach, she saw RV's and trailers attached to pickup trucks.

She remembered Big John saying that squatters, who managed without electricity and running water, could be seen where the road ended, living along the beach throughout the year. The island narrowed at this point to less than one hundred yards, and gradually widened again over the next couple of miles to around a quarter mile wide. The sand was wet and compact, so it was easy to navigate for vehicles with four-wheel drives. He also said the squatters were peaceful, and as long as they didn't bother anyone, no one paid them a bother.

The breeze had kicked up, and the waves were smacking the shore. She noticed the flag missing from her private island. *Police must have taken that for evidence.* What with the cloud cover, she could barely see the sand bar.

She started walking toward the parked RV's for help, but quickly changed her mind. *Don't bother them—they don't bother you.* Jules hit the picture of Big John on her friends list and waited.

"Yo," he said, answering on the second ring.

"Sorry. Did I make you spill your beer again?"

"No," he said. "But I worry when you take off like that. So, what's up?"

"I'm going to need a tow. The Ferrari is kind of stuck in the sand at the end of 100."

"How stuck?"

"Twenty feet."

"No problem. Give me half an hour."

"Jules, grab me a bag of zip ties from the glove compartment," Big John ordered, as he kicked Tony's legs to spread them apart.

Jules returned a minute later with the bag opened, and a twenty-seven inch Plastic Zip-Tie Handcuff in her hand.

"Put your gun on him while I handcuff him."

Jules handed him two more for Tony's ankles, and then turn around when she heard the police sirens blaring. "Here's Chief Smith and his posse," she said.

When Smitty got out of his squad car with his gun drawn, Big John removed his foot from Tony's butt, and tucked his H & K in the small of his back. Jules did the same with her gun.

"Thank you, Jules. I'll take it from here."

"Where are you taking him?" Jules asked. "I want to talk to him."

"Your part's done, Jules."

"Chief—"

"Damn girl. I'm booking him at the station. He'll be locked up in the temporary holding facility until he's transferred to Cameron County Jail in Brownsville tomorrow."

"When can I see him?"

"You don't give up, do you?"

"Nope!" Jules said, grinning ear to ear.

"After six tonight," Chief Smith said. "Call first. Don't just show up, or I'll have a room for you, too."

"Fine." Jules started for the Ferrari when she remembered she needed a tow. "Big John, how about you winch me out of the sand.

Chief Smith, his posse, and Tony were long gone by the time the Ferrari was freed from the sand and wiped down. "Thanks Big John. I'll meet you back at the house," she said. "I need to come up with a believable story for Jack."

Jules left with Big John behind her. No racing this time. She had to think. As she drove by Island Adventure Park, she slowed down and looked for the mayor. She thought of stopping when a black Porsche Turbo pulled up at the entrance. She thought better of it, and continued driving.

Dr. Bryce Kellogg in her Kala Kellingworth persona tailed Jules from a safe distance. The Porsche had enough power to keep the speeding Ferrari in sight. Bryce had some concerns regarding what Jules had gathered from her snooping. She was on Route 100 when Jules put on her show racing through traffic. The opportunity was too good to miss.

She rented an ATV at Island Adventure Park, and drove along the shore to the end of Route 100. She watched as Jules combed the beach, and could imagine how she ended up near the shoreline. When Jules camped

out by the Ferrari after making a call, she assumed it was for a tow, and put her binoculars down. But when Tony made his appearance, she pulled her gun. Concerned for Jules safety, she was prepared to take Tony out.

Jules was full of surprises, she thought when she saw Jules pull a Glock on him. She was relieved when Big John arrived, and left to return the ATV. She watched from the returns window as three cop cars sped by the park. Bryce was sure Tony was going to jail, and would take the rap. All her attention could now be focused on Dr. Russell and Dr. Davenport.

Jules saw Jack pacing back and forth when she reached the top of the bridge to Anna's island. *This isn't going to fare well,* she thought. Jack's demeanor told her he was pissed. "Suck it up, Champ," she said, and drove to the garage.

Jack put his hands on the Ferrari's door and stared at Jules. He looked cool and calm, but a muscle near his jaw joint twitched. "I can't wait to hear this story," he said. "You are supposed to be at the research center. Roy called me an hour ago to say you were AWOL."

"I told him that I was going to miss the lab," she said.

"You didn't tell me."

Jules smiled. "You didn't ask," she said. "You know: Don't tell, don't ask."

"Not funny, Jules, I'm grounding you."

Jules moved his hands so she could get out of the car. "I'll be in my room," she said, and kept on walking.

"No. You'll be in the den. I want to hear everything. No bullshit this time."

"Fine," she replied over her shoulder.

"Chief Smith called—" Jack paused as Big John pulled up in his truck.

Jules stopped and turned back toward Jack. She gave a thumbs up to Big John.

"He says you plan on going to see that Tony character at the jail."

"What else did he say?"

"He wasn't too happy, but he said to tell you nice job."

Jules turned back toward the house. A smile radiated from her face.

"Don't go patting yourself on the back, young lady," Jack said. A sly grin appearing on his face. "BADDAY clocked you at over two-hundred and twenty miles per hour. Now I have to see how much damage you've caused to Anna's pride and joy."

"I already checked it out . . . she's fine."

"Knock off the speeding," Jack said, and then let out a hardy laugh. "There's no mistaking who you're related to. Damn, you're as reckless as Buck."

Big John moseyed over toward Jack—his head down. "Sorry Jack. The damn kid is elusive."

"Don't worry about it," Jack said. "Dinner is at eighteen-hundred. Then we're all going to see Chief Smith."

24

**SPI Police Station
Monday Night April 8th**

The holding cells—all eight of them—had occupants. Tony Labarbera had the interview room all to himself, and he was the only one making noise. Everyone else, holdovers from spring break and John Waite, the town drunk, were all eating dinner.

"I want my lawyer," Tony said to the empty room. He figured someone was watching and listening in on him.

But Chief Smith had blocked him out hours ago. Tony would get his one call when the Chief was good and ready. With his feet on his desk, a Mexican cigar in one hand, and three fingers of Dewars in the other, he was finally kicking back from a long day. It was a little after seven, and he still hadn't heard from Jules. *Lucky me,* he thought. *Maybe Jack had talked some sense into her after all.*

The phone on his desk rang, black, with push buttons. He answered the phone. "SPIPD, Chief Smith here."

"It's me Chief. I'm outside with Jack and Big John. Open up."

"Jules, I thought I told you to call first."

"I did."

"I meant before you left home. Kind of give me a chance to get out of here first."

"Sorry, Chief."

"Give me a minute, and stop calling me Chief."

"Yes Chief."

When Smitty unlocked the door Jules handed him a brown paper bag that was stapled closed.

"What's this?"

Jules kept walking toward the holding area. "A present, go ahead and open it," she said.

A guard stopped her, and pointed her toward the Chiefs office.

Jack reached out his hand. Chief Smith put the cigar in his mouth and accepted the handshake. "Sorry Smitty," Jack said. "I tried, but she's stubborn . . . just like her grandfather."

"Me, too, Smitty," Big John said, giving him a big Texas grin.

"Alright, let's get this over with."

Smitty opened the bag, and removed the bottle of sixty year old Macallan as he walked into his office and took a seat. He quickly shoved the bottle of Dewars in his bottom drawer, and pulled out three rock glasses. He pulled the fancy stopper from the bottle, and poured a couple of fingers in a fresh glass. "Guys?"

Jack and Big John nodded.

Chief Smith looked toward Jules and squinted his eyes "This doesn't change anything, Jules," he said. "You still got half an hour."

Jules stood and smiled. She placed a Partagus 150 Churchill—a seven inch by fifty-two inch ring—a tad bit less than an inch in diameter by the bottle of Macallan. "Bet this does."

Chief Smith picked up the cigar and sniffed it. He looked at Jules and smiled. "You're learning fast kid. Take your time with the scumbag." He put out the cheap Mexican cigar, and lit the two-hundred dollar one. "Hey, Jules. Where did you happen to find one of these?"

Jules who was already heading to the holding cell turned, looking back at the Chief. "Grandpa Buck's stash."

"Hope there's more," he said. "I figure you owe me . . . big time."

Jack got up from the chair, and downed his drink. "I better go with her."

The Chief stood, too. "We'll all go. This should be interesting."

The guard opened the cell door and pointed at the chair cemented to the floor. "Sit," he said. "Arm's out front." The guard shackled Tony to the chair. "He's safe."

The Chief, Jules, Jack, and Big John all grabbed a seat around Tony. The guard stood by the door.

The Chief talked first. "This young lady is going to ask you some questions. Answer them."

"I didn't do anything . . . I swear."

"Tony . . . just remember that Texas has the death penalty. So anything you say that helps out in the investigation will be taken into consideration."

"Listen, all I did was have sex with the girls."

"Those girls were plied with drugs, and had deep lesions on their necks," Jules said.

"What?"

"You choked them to death," Jules replied.

"Okay, maybe it got a little rough, but they were alive when I left them. And I'll tell you something else: I left them both near Island Adventure Park. How did they end up where they were?"

"That's what we want to know," Chief Smith said. "So talk."

"I swear, I'm being set up. There was a woman who I think was following me around. I saw her several times.

"What's her name," Chief Smith asked.

"Kara or Kala something. Her card is in my wallet."

"How did you get her card, if you thought she was following you around?" Jules asked.

212

"When I heard the police scanner mention a dead girl at Isla Grand Beach Resort, I went to look for myself."

"Police scanners are illegal, Tony," Chief Smith said. "Hey Steve, do me a favor and go get Tony's wallet."

All eyes followed the guard as he left.

The Chief turned back toward Tony. "Continue."

"I didn't cut that girl, or stab her, I swear."

When the guard returned with the wallet, the Chief emptied the contents.

"That one there," Tony said, motioning with his nose."

"Kala Kellingworth, Entrepreneur," the Chief announced.

"That's it," Tony said. "That's her. She was following me."

Jules pulled out her R-CAT and ran a search. "A Kala Kellingworth happens to have a suite at the Seabreeze III Resort," she said, and then paused a moment before adding. "It's owned by her father. Tony you have to do better than that."

"It's her. I swear."

"Smitty, I'm done here," Jules said. "Lock him up and throw away the key."

Jules stood and walked out of the room. She was far from done. The picture of Kala on the search she ran matched with several of the pictures she had from her analysis. But something about Kala looked familiar."

"Come on guys," she said. "Let's go. Thanks Chief."

213

He was going to say don't call me Chief, but thought to leave well enough alone. "Okay, Jules, that's it right? No more snooping. . . right?"

"You bet, Smitty." Jules let out a giggle while leaving.

"Why don't I believe you," he replied, shaking his head. "Okay, Steve, lock him back up. I'm going home, too."

Upon returning home, Jules complained she was tired and was heading off to bed. She began running searches the second she entered her room. Kala Kellingworth was rich in her own right. She was a world traveler, and listed as an executive of Kellingworth Enterprises.

Dr. Bryce Kellogg's name appeared under known associates. They had been roommates in college.

Jules remembered Bryce had moved to America when she was eight. The file didn't go back any further, but it did say she originated from England. Jules ran a fuzzy search on any connection between the names Kellogg, Russell, Davenport, and Kellingworth. While the search was running, she left her room and slowly crept down the stairs to get a drink and snack. When she passed the den, Jack and Emma were cuddling. *How cute*, she thought, and continued on to the kitchen.

"Jules, where are you going?" Jack asked.

214

"You don't miss anything, do you," Jules returned. "I'm just getting a drink and snack. Is that alright with you?"

"Thought you were going to bed?"

"Can't sleep," she lied.

"What are you up to, Jules?"

"Nothing. Honest," Jules said, and then giggled. "Maybe you two ought to go to bed."

"Grab me a Corona and fruit," Jack said. "If you don't mind, that is."

"Emma, do you want anything?"

"No, honey. Thank you."

Jules brought Jack his beer, and looked closely at the two of them. *They do make a good couple*, she thought. *Good for them. Now, if only I could find someone, without freaking out.*

The search was finished by the time Jules returned to her room. The fuzzy search nailed it. Seems there was a partnership in England between a Dr. Winston Kyllehog, Dr. Russell, and Dr. Davenport. All three were quantum physicists. Jules read all the articles, then ran further searches. The last search produced the answers she was looking for: Dr. Kyllehog had a daughter named Bryce. He committed suicide after his patent for a touch screen device was allegedly stolen.

"Bam!" Jules said, maybe a tad bit loudly. She stared at Bryce's name on the screen. *Bryce's mother must have changed their last name when they came to America. Tony may be a piece of crap, and he did belong in jail, but he didn't kill Sandy and Miffy. Now my work really begins.* She shut down the

215

computer and lay back on her pillow. The video feeds from the CIA satellite played in her mind.

The Seabreeze III was just north of Coca-Cola Beach at the Isla Grand Beach Resort. She remembered seeing Bryce in the parking lot at the Seabreeze, thinking nothing of it at the time. In fact she wasn't really looking at Bryce at all. *But tomorrow I will*, she thought and drifted off to sleep.

25

Anna's Island
Tuesday Morning April 9th

The buzz coming from Jules R-CAT at five a.m. wrestled her from her dream; although her dream remained fresh in her mind. Hell everything was. The toughest part of having an eidetic mind was controlling your thoughts, and staying in the present.

Jules put herself in Bryce's shoes.

What would I do if it were mom or dad—Buck or Anna?

Would I exact revenge?

Would I kill?

Jules tried to wash away the dream. Steam from the shower filled the bathroom. *Stay in the present.*

She started to brush her teeth, and wiped a layer of brume from the mirror on the medicine cabinet. The face staring back was not hers. It was Bryce's. Her lips were moving, but no sound escaped.

"What? Damn it," Jules said to the vision.

The vision mouthed the words again. *You would kill, too.*

Jules flung the bathroom door open, and jumped into her bed. She pulled the covers over her head and screamed. "Stop!"

"Jules! Open the door!" Jack shouted, while banging on her door.

She pulled the covers from her head and tried to sound like she was in control of her emotions. "It's okay, Jack . . . just a bad dream."

"Open the door!"

"It's okay," she repeated, a little more calmly this time. She got up from the bed and wrapped herself in a bath robe. A moment later, she opened the door. "I'm fine."

"If you're fine," he said. "Explain to me how you dream out loud in the shower."

"Did I wake you? I'm sorry."

"It's not that. I've been up since five. I was going to surprise you with a nice breakfast."

Jules wrapped her arms around Jack, buried her head into his chest, and squeezed him tightly. "I'll be okay, Jack.

It's just my mind spinning a million miles per hour. Everything is popping up at the same time."

"Maybe you should stay home today and relax. We can go to the gun range later."

Jules looked into Jacks eyes and released her arms. "You sure know the way to a woman's heart."

He shook off her flirt. "Coffee's ready—Anna's special blend," he said. "I'll go start the bacon, and you can decide how you want your eggs when you come down. Now get dressed. What would Emma think if she saw us?"

Jules laughed hard. "Thanks, I needed that."

Jack left her, closing the door behind him.

The mixed aroma of sizzling bacon and rich Russian coffee welcomed Jules as she entered the kitchen. Jack had just placed a stack of slightly toasted tortillas in a ceramic server designed to keep them warm.

"Nice touch, Jack."

"I can read you like a book, Jules. Scrambled or fried?"

"Scrambled."

Jules poured herself a mug of coffee and refilled Jacks. "I'm going to the morning lecture, but I'd like to hit the range and simulator after lunch."

"Call me. I'll meet you there."

Jules left after breakfast. Her and Jack engaged in small talk about Tony, but the dreams were never brought up.

Jules was the first student in the lecture hall, and she immediately dove into the CIA video archives. She set the search criteria for Bryce and Kala. While the program was running, she hacked into the NTSB—National Transportation Safety Board database. The NTSB—an independent government agency—was tasked with investigating civil transportation accidents. In that role, the NTSB investigated and reported on aviation accidents and incidents, including cases of hazardous materials released during transportation.

The NTSB also had access to every logged passenger flight, and their manifests. Jules ran a search on Bryce and Kala, and found what she was looking for. A private jet owned by Kellingworth Enterprises filed a flight plan for Sunday morning, April 7th from Brownsville SPI Airport to Las Lenas, Argentina. *Kala had to be on that flight.* Bryce had a Sunday morning flight to George Bush Intercontinental Airport in Houston on Southwest Air, with a three hour layover before heading on to New York's LaGuardia airport.

The flight was for show, thought Jules. Bryce never boarded the flight to New York. But a Kala Kellingworth returned to Brownsville SPI International Airport on an afternoon flight from George Bush Intercontinental Airport in Houston on Southwest Airlines.

Jules ran another search through the credit card database, and Kala Kellingworth's American Express card popped up several times at the finest restaurants in Las Lenas.

Nice move, Bryce, thought Jules. *Covered your ass pretty good.*

Jules knew what she was looking for now, and amended her search to include the Seabreeze III Resort. She bookmarked every hit, and began playing the videos looking for anything that would indicate someone besides Bryce. The search was futile. *I tried Bryce*, thought Jules. *But everything points to you.*

"Whatchadoin," Jai said, dragging out the syllables. He sat down next to Jules.

Oh, this is going to suck big time, thought Jules. *Just what I needed: Jai blabbering to his uncle.* Jules turned toward him as she closed her laptop. "Nothing . . . I'm just running some searches." She continued to make small talk with Jai as the room began to fill.

"Hey, nice job on nailing that Tony Labarbera guy," Jai said. "Did you know he worked here?"

"Yeah, the perv has been eyeing me all week," she replied. "Chief Smith says he has enough to charge Tony with the murders of Sandy and Miffy." Jules wanted to change the subject. "What do you think of Dr. Lyn Alexander?"

221

Jai didn't bite.

"Uncle Roy says Sandy and Miffy's fathers are flying in tomorrow."

"Yeah, I heard that, too," Jules said as the room lights began to dim. "Alright, hush now."

Dr. Lyn Alexander began her lecture.

The Tiki bar was packed when Jules and Jack returned from the gun range and flight simulator room. It was a quarter after five, and members of the elite security force, men and woman dressed in camouflage snake-eater BDU's, had just gotten off their shift and were being entertained by Big John.

Jack had pushed Jules hard on the Hughes simulator. She was dog tired, but her landings were good enough to pass the licensing test.

"How'd you do?" Big John asked.

Jules pointed a thumb over her shoulder. "Ask Jack . . . he tried to kill me with hurricanes and complete white-outs.

Big John nodded toward Jack who had a big ass smile on his face. "She did good," Jack said. "Gunny's going to get her a license."

Jules sat at the bar next to Jai and Roy. "Hey, big guy, how about surprising me with something fancy? She quickly added. "Without alcohol in it, please."

"Coming right up," Big John replied, and then added. "You guys hungry."

"Yes, but I want to change it up a little bit," Jules replied. "I'd like to try that new sushi place Kabuki's."

"Sounds like fun," Roy said. "But Jai and I have to get back to the lab and work on the CIA satellite programs."

Jai put his hand over Jules'. He was surprised when she didn't try to move it. "Maybe we could get together later—"

Jules looked into his eyes. "We'll see," she said, cutting him off.

"—if you're not busy that is," he continued.

"I'll call you when we get back," Jules said, and Jai didn't push any further.

"Sorry Jules," Jack said. "I can't make it either. Emma needs help at the lab tonight. I was going to grab a quick bite here, have a couple of beers with the team, and then head back over."

"Fine then," Jules said. "It's me and you, Big John. How about we take the Hunter out and sail over to Kabuki's? We can dock at the Boardwalk."

Jules had seen the Hunter docked by Bucks beach house when her and Jack left the research center. Her plan was coming together, and no one was the wiser.

"I'm going to take a nap," Jules said. "How about we meet at seven? Maybe catch at nice sunset on the Laguna Madre before we have diner."

"That's a date," Big John said. "Give me some time to get cleaned up."

223

Jules finished her virgin strawberry daiquiri, and then left the Tiki bar for her room. She had a few more sections of video to review. Earlier in the day, she had watched Bryce and Kala come and go from the Seabreeze III on several occasions. One piece of footage showed Kala leaving, and then Bryce entering the resort five minutes later. Ten minutes after Bryce arrived, another person who looked exactly like Kala left the resort. Jules put a bookmark on that footage, and then went to the footage of Kala originally leaving the resort. She followed Kala all the way to the hanger where her private jet was kept at Brownsville SPI International Airport. *No way it was Kala the second time.*

The second person leaving the resort was not Kala. The software Greg had on his system was a copy of BADDAY's tracking system, and she tagged the individual who she believed was Bryce. Jules ran advance biometrics on the individual, and did the same with the footage of Bryce she had viewed earlier.

Although it wasn't even a sixty percent match, Jules was convinced that Bryce was parading around at night as Kala. She would turn this information over to Anna when she got back.

Back in her bedroom, Jules replayed the footage from Saturday night and Sunday morning. She just had to see it again on tape, not from her memory.

Convinced she was doing the right thing, she shut down her laptop and took a shower. With just a towel around her head, she air dried, and set out the clothes she would be wearing to dinner. Jules also rolled up the black bodysuit she would wear later that night, and then tucked it in her *go* bag. She grabbed the GSP/IPS jammer she had lifted from Roy, who had conveniently left it on the bar's table, and put it in the *go* bag, as well. She had never tested it, but tonight she would get the chance to.

Tonight I'm going dark, she thought, and looked at the bodysuit she soon would be wearing. A smile spread across her face. *Major league dark. Just like Grandpa Buck. And I will deal with the consequences. Just like he would.*

GENE HILGREEN

26

Kabuki's Restaurant
Wednesday April 10th

Jules parked her golf cart by the front deck of Buck's beach house. Halfway up the stairs to the deck she was summoned.

"Yo, over here," Big John said. He was on the Hunter popping open a Corona. "I got some water for you, but we need more ice. Grab a bag from the freezer."

Jules started for the kitchen, and stopped when sunlight from a rear window lit up the hallway to the west. The walls on both sides were lined with framed photos. The one wall had photos of core members of the Corporation taken at parties and sporting events. But the other wall seemed to be dedicated to Jules. Pictures from major gymnastic events from the time she was eight up until the national championships. There were also pictures of her receiving her degrees. Hand written placards were under each photo, and Jules recognized the scribble to be that of Big John.

So I have a secret admirer.

Jules pulled herself away from memory lane and grabbed two bags of ice from the freezer. Her gate had an extra skip to it as she pranced to the Hunter.

"Jules, release the bow lines before you come aboard." Big John jumped down on the dock to remove the dock lines, and guided the boat as Jules boarded. She went straight to the wheelhouse, bringing out a big Texas smile from Big John. "Take her out," he said. "She's all yours."

Jules took command of the wheel, and looked over at Big John who was downing his beer. "So tell me about the photos."

Big John's perpetual tan turned a shade redder. He popped another Corona and took a swig before he looked back toward Jules. "Hey," he said as a grin spread across his face. "You're like the daughter I never had, and—"

Jules interrupted him before he got all mushy. She knew that Big John would do anything for her. "It's okay big guy. . . I know, and thank you."

The wind was light, and it took the better part of forty minutes to tack and sail south to the boardwalk, but

228

they were moored in time for the spectacular sunset at seven-fifty.

"Okay, Jules, let's batten down the hatches and get some raw fish," Big John said. It was just an expression. Big John wasn't concern about water getting into the sailing palace, but he was concerned about miscreants coming aboard and helping themselves to the goods.

The best entertainment at any sushi restaurant comes from sitting at the carving bar, and that was where Jules and Big John sat.

"What will it be, young lady" said the head chef with an obvious Japanese and Texan twang.

"Surprise me," Jules said. "Combination of sushi and sashimi, I'm starving."

The chef looked toward Big John.

"Same here," he said. "And I'll have a large sake, too—hot."

For the next two hours they ate everything the chef put in front of them. When Jules was finally full, she gave the server her credit card and turned toward Big John.

"Give me a minute," she said. "I am going to hit the ladies room."

When Jules returned she was dressed in black—head to toe, and her hair was up in a tight bun.

Big John took one look at her and shook his head. "No way," was all he managed to say.

"Yes," said Jules.

"What?" Big John said.

"I'll explain outside," she said. "Follow me."

Jules reached into her go bag and hit the switch on the jammer. From this point on she was dark. Big John followed her along the beach in the direction of the Seabreeze III Resort.

The sun had set hours ago, and as dusk turn to darkness the first full moon of the month made its appearance. Tall ornamental beach grasses shrouded a shadowy figure near the supply hut that separated the pool area from the beach. A shimmering pool of luminous light broke through the marine layer and splashed across the sand.

Big John was the first to see her, as the moonbeams lit up her silhouette for the scantest of seconds. Her dark brown hair and bullet like eyes stopped him in his tracks. Trance-like he stared as the light glittered across her body—highlighting every curve under her black form-fitting bodysuit. Her right arm fully extended, pointing at him and Jules.

Light flickered off the long barrel that extended from her hand. The most beautiful woman he had ever seen was packing 9mm heat and her stance proved she knew how to use it.

The lump in his throat worked its way through his body, and his first couples of words were incoherent. He gathered himself and repeated them. "Stay close." After regrouping, he pointed a small Heckler & Koch P7M8 pistol toward the figure.

Jules saw her, too. But it was Big John's reaction that scared her. She shook his arm. "Get it together big guy . . . she's just a woman."

"That is not just a woman, and I'm more worried about you."

A distinct spit broke the silence of the night, and shards of wood sprinkled from the seawall a foot from Big John's head.

When Jules turned back to the beach the mysterious figure, who she believed was Dr. Bryce Kellogg—was gone. "Let's split up. Go right, I'll go left."

"I don't think that's wise, Jules."

Jules pulled her baby Glock from her waistband. "It's wise." She handed him a palm sized device. Jules had one just like it attached to the neckline of her body suit. "It's a walky-talky. Keep it on speaker so I know where you are. Let's go find her. Now!" Jules turned and ran to the left.

Big John watched as she disappeared into the shadows. He didn't like the idea of Jules running off all cocky like. "Jules," he groaned to himself. Then he simply shook his head and cursed as he followed her instructions. "Damn her."

Jules stayed in the shadows of the six foot high, raised boardwalk and seawall that ran the length of the Seabreeze III resort. She climbed a few steps at each stairway that accessed the beach and stole a glance of the outer pool area. It was always clear. "That woman is good, I'll give her that."

She caught a glimpse of a few guests mingling at the Tiki bar. There was still no sign of the woman in black and so she continued on to the next hotel, circling back through the pool area.

Big John ran to the end of the wall, and made a right. He continued into the parking area but didn't see anyone. He pulled out his walky-talky to alert Jules.

The woman in black left the shadows and yelled, "You in the hat. Drop the gun, hands up high, and turn around—slowly."

Big John turned to the voice, heavy breathing emanated from the device in his left hand. *Jules was running,* he thought. *I have to warn her.* The first dart hit him and stunned him as he mouthed Jules' name.

The woman in black watched as the man in the hat fell backward. She reloaded the gun. "Sorry, Big John," she said, and pointed the gun at his chest. She waved the gun back and forth across his torso. "I thought we had something going, but you know too much." She aimed and fired the second dart at his heart. This one was meant to terminate him.

A garbled yowl squawked from Jules' communication device, followed up by her name.

"Big John, where are you?"

Nothing for a couple of seconds, and then another voice began talking. Jules knew who the voice belonged to.

"Big John!" Jules screamed, as she ran back to the beach hut where she had last seen him.

She found him three minutes later propped against the wall. Darts from a high powered weapon protruded from his chest. Jules fell to her knees and felt for a pulse. He was out and barely breathing, but miraculously still alive. She reached into her pocket for the jammer and her R-CAT. The R-CAT fell to the sand as a dart hit her in the middle of her back. The impact caused her to fall forward into Big Johns' chest. Her mind began to blur immediately. She knew the R-CAT would be disabled by BADDAY, and useless to anyone, but the jammer was different. She turned it off, and shoved it as deep as she could into the sand under Big John. A second dart smacked into her back, and her mind went blank.

Bryce left her cover and assessed the two bodies. Big John would be a problem with his size and weight, but she had a winch and lift on the truck she rented. Getting his body onto the boat would take some time. Jules on the other hand would fit perfectly into the oversized luggage bag that Kala had for moving her personal treasures.

Bryce moved her truck as close as she could to the bodies. She rolled Big John into a crate, and attached the winch. Within minutes his body was in the truck bed and covered. As she neared Jules a red flashing light faintly discerned itself through the sand. She pointed a high beam pen light at the location and carefully brushed away the sand. She recognized the device immediately.

"Thank you, Jules," she whispered. Next she placed Jules' limp body in the oversized Tumi expandable wheeled case. With her knees pressed against her chest, she fit in perfectly.

Ten minutes later she was wheeling Jules into the elevator at the Seabreeze III Resort. The woman at the concierge desk never batted an eyelash. Jules would be out for several hours, but Bryce, taped her mouth shut and secured her in the guest room, anyway. Now she had to contend with disposing of Big John.

27

Seabreeze III Resort
Wednesday night April 10th

Jules' life flashed before her eyes, but she wasn't awake. She knew every scene, every event as it played out. A movie trailer of her life on full throttle, and she couldn't stop it or change anything.

Her childhood friends—the few she had. Birthday parties, gymnastic practice, and more practice. Scenes from school, all her schools, and special classes she'd attended flashed by her mind's eye. The studying sessions with her mom, and her time spent studying with Anna.

Angel's Landing brought a smile to her face. All the 'don't tell mom moments' with Grandpa Buck, Jack, and Anna. *Yeah, I want to be like Buck and Anna.* Shooting guns and rifles every chance she could in the range with Buck. Then there was Anna letting her take control of the Hughes. Yeah, a constant flash of 'don't tell Mom moments'—that had been her life.

Then there was the National Championships, and she was smiling.

Why? You blew it, remember? But something nagged at the back of her mind, causing her to experience a sharp pain in her head. Jules continued to watch her life's short, clip-like movies, and they revealed how terribly short and solitary her life really had been. Tears began pooling in her eyes.

A loud bang roused her from her visions. Jules opened her eyes to darkness and confusion, and then it came back to her. *Bryce shot me. Well at least I'm alive—poor Big John.*

She tried to move, but couldn't—her arms and legs were tied up. She tried biting at the tape across her mouth to loosen it, but it was fastened very well and she finally gave up the attempt. Her head hurt, and she closed her eyes. Jules' mind went right back to her floor exercise routine at the Nationals, playing it over and over for her until she realized something.

OMG—I blew the National Championships. Those weren't mistakes I was making; I did those things on purpose. I was happy and content with the vaulting title. I wanted to be right here, right now. I wanted to start a new life. I don't want to be a gymnast or scientist; I want to be like Grandpa.

The sound of breaking glass pulled Jules back into consciousness. A door slamming into a wall knocked a picture off the wall.

No. I want both. I want to be a scientist and help humanity. I also want to be like Grandpa Buck, and stop those who want to do evil.

Her eyes began to adjust to the darkness. She pulled at the straps holding her.

What would Grandpa Buck do?

Music played from another room. The banging stopped, and now Jules could hear drawers opening and closing. Then a loud crash, like wood splintering and marbles rolling on the floor. *A chest*, thought Jules, *and jewelry spilling across the floor.*

She heard someone talking, but no one answering.

"Where's the money, bitch?"

Jules' head hurt bad. "Clear the mechanism," she said under her breath. Her mind cleared and she rested. *How do I get out of this predicament? Think, damn it. What would Buck do?*

A foul taste had formed in her mouth, causing her to choke on her own phlegm. She tried to assess her whereabouts, but as she looked around the dark room, all she saw were fine lines of moonlight peeking in from the drawn, heavy curtains.

Her arms were tied to the rear styles of the chair backing, and her legs were bound to the chair legs with double flex cuffs. Her toes could feel the feet of the chair. She took notice that she was in a comfortable, heavy

Victorian era chair. She found out just how heavy when she tried to move the chair by wiggling back and forth.

"You're awake," said a voice from another room.

Bryce, thought Jules. The thought was confirmed when Bryce, who could have passed for Kala's twin entered the room, and turned on a desk lamp.

Bryce pointed a Glock with a suppressor attached at Jules. "Don't make me use this," she said, and pulled the tape away from Jules' mouth.

"Why, Bryce?" Jules asked.

"You wouldn't understand."

"I know about your father, Bryce. You don't have to do this. We can help you."

"If you know about my father . . . then you know why I *have* to do this. They must pay for everything they've done."

"But Bryce—"

"But nothing, Jules. I like you a lot . . . it's the only reason you're not with your bodyguard."

"What did you do to Big John?"

Bryce looked away from Jules—never answering, and cleared off a space on the dresser.

Jules' eyes were on fire but she didn't want to provoke Bryce, at least not yet. Jules stole a cautious glance at Bryce. The woman's deep brown eyes burned with a fire and intelligence that Jules had rarely seen in anyone but Buck, Anna, or Jack. She watched Bryce put a small box on the dresser.

"How did you know it was me?"

"Jules, for someone as intelligent as you, sometimes you're blind to the obvious. Your arrogance will be the death of you one day."

"What are you talking about?"

"Oh, Jules, please—the friendship bracelet?"

"You're tracking me?"

"Not just you—Big John and Kala have one, too."

"What's that device on the dresser?"

Bryce looked away from her and walked toward the dresser. "Who else knows, Jules?"

"What did you do to Big John?"

"Stay out of this, Jules . . . for your own good. Now answer the question: Who else knows?"

"Anna."

Bryce smiled and ripped off three pieces of Duct tape. "I think not. If Anna knew, you wouldn't be here."

"What's the device?"

"It's my back up plan. I get away safe, you live. Simple as that."

Jules bit Bryce's hand as she tried to apply the tape to her mouth.

Bryce smacked her hard in the face. "Stay still!"

"I will hunt you down and—"

"And what, Jules?"

Jules paused a moment, before blurting out, "Kill you."

Bryce placed Jules' Glock next to the device. "Just as I thought. Here's your Glock, not that you'll get to use it."

She turned off the light, and started toward the bedroom door. She pressed a button on the remote she was carrying and the device began flashing. "I'm leaving now. You have twenty-nine minutes and forty-five seconds to live. Let's see if you're as good as you think you are."

28

Angel's Landing, Aspen Colorado
Wednesday April 10th

Anna looked out at Aspen Highland through the glass wall of the library as snow began accumulating on the illuminated back deck. She needed something to calm her nerves, as she impatiently tapped her R-CAT against her thigh. She was not happy with Jack's latest report.

Three hours had passed since Jules went dark, and she received the initial SOS call from Roy. Jack had retraced her movements from the time she had set sail from the island to the moment she went dark at Kabuki's. He was at Kubuki's and had just finished grilling the proprietor and staff. Jules, dressed in a black bodysuit, along with Big John had left together shortly after nine.

241

"She can't have just disappeared," Anna said, tears dripping down her check.

"I'll find her," Jack said. "But it gets worse. Roy says that his demo jammer is missing."

"Damn her," Anna said, choking back her tears. "Whatever it takes, Jack. Buck and I are leaving shortly. I'll call you when we're wheels up," she said, slightly butchering the W's. She quickly disconnected the call. Anna pushed through the glass doors of the solarium and walked toward the lap pool.

A few rays of moonlight emanated through the skylights, otherwise the solarium was dark. It had an eerie aura about it, and Anna found the silence of the room disquieting. When the doors closed, Creedence Clearwater Revivals, *Fortunate Son,* could be heard blaring from the speakers as Buck and another man swam lap after lap in the heated pool. Buck's pace quickened with each stroke, and the man in the adjacent lane kept pace. Anna knew that the song was Buck's favorite, and he always played it for inspiration. When he reached the pool wall where she was standing she shouted his name.

He slapped the wall, flipped and propelled in the other direction. She screamed his name again, but to no avail. The second man had heard the scream and climbed out from the pool.

"Jameson, how's he doing?"

Jameson Davidssen, Senator of the great state of California smiled at Anna, and then he shifted his eyes toward his father back in the pool. "Not bad for an old dog."

They both watched as Buck reached the other end of the pool and flipped around. He switched his stroke to a butterfly. His upper torso rose from the water with each stroke. She screamed his name again, and this time he stopped. Anna backed away as he grabbed the lip on the edge, and in one swift movement, rocketed out of the pool.

Anna looked at the scarred bullet hole in his thigh. Her eyes continued moving up his body and she saw other souvenirs of his trade. Her gaze locked on the water dripping from his massive chest as his muscles contracted and flexed with each breath. The over-sized tattoo of the American flag centered in the middle of his chest appeared to wave.

Anna smiled, and grabbing him tightly, kissed him hard. She suddenly released her grip and looked into his eyes. *God and Old Glory aside*, she thought. *The look in Buck's eyes told her someone was going to die today.*

"Get dressed," she said. "The truck is packed, and Sarge is taking us to the airport."

"Anna, I can't go," Jameson said. "The boss wants me in DC. Said she is grooming me as her VP in the next election."

"Damn that Char," Anna said. "Work, work, work, that's all she does."

"Look who's calling the kettle black," Buck said.

"Think I'll stay out of this one," Jameson interrupted. "Call me when you know what's going on."

Jameson was not a member of The Corporation and was on a need to know basis. But that would change soon if he became VP. Char and Anna thought he was ready to be brought into the fold. Buck thought he was safer sticking to politics.

Big John woke up freezing, groggy, and in pain. His first thought was to find Jules. The LED on his watch told him that more than three hours had passed since he'd blacked out. He couldn't see anything else. His hand moved to his chest and he felt something protruding from it. He looked down and noticed a dart sticking out from him. That dart was meant to kill him, but it impaled and stuck fast into his Navy Seal dog tags that never left his neck. Those tags saved his life.

It took him another ten minutes to gather his bearings. That's when he realized he was in a deep ice chest. Relief splashed across his face when he retrieved the K-Bar from his boot. Another hour would pass before he could free himself from the chest.

The lights of South Padre Island were the first thing he saw after he kicked the door off the boat's cabin where he had been stashed. Making his way off the dock, he found Greg's dune buggy parked right where he'd left it a couple of days ago. With reckless abandon, he drove straight to the research center. His only thought was to find Jules.

"Call Jack," Big John said to the security guard manning the front door.

"He's upstairs with Dr. Singh," the guard said.

"Call him anyway, and tell him I'm coming up."

Jack met him at Roy's office door. "What happened? Where's Jules?"

Big John gave a detailed description of the night, including Jules's transformation into a ninja. He explained Jules had been out the door before he could stop her, and the events leading up until the present.

"Jack—I did everything I could to stop her."

"Nobody is doubting you big guy," the look on Jacks face was sincere. "Where was she headed?" Jack asked.

"Toward the Isla Grand Beach Resort."

"Well then let's roll," Jack said.

Jules started counting the second the door had slammed shut. Ten minutes had passed, Bryce had not returned, and she was still strapped in the chair. She pulled and twisted her arms to no avail. She could not break the grip of the thick plastic cuffs. The same result occurred when she strained against the ties on her legs. Suddenly, she had an idea.

Damn, this is going to hurt.

She began to rock back and forth, careful not to fall backward. Her goal was to fall forward, not smashing her face too hard. On the fourth rock she forced her body forward with all her might. The chair teetered forward and fell. She tucked her chin so her forehead would take the brunt of the fall.

"Shit!"

Jules rested for a few seconds, then arched her back and flexed her knees. The feet of the chair lifted off of the ground. She then collapsed her body forcing all of her weight on the feet of the chair legs. She continued the process over and over, until her knees couldn't take it anymore. She rested a few seconds, and then continued the torture until she couldn't take the pain any longer.

On the fourth try, the right foot of the chair began to crack. She rested and started again. On her next try it cracked a little more. After one last desperate effort, the right foot finally broke away from the chair leg, and she wriggled until her leg came free from the Ziploc and chair.

She straightened her right leg out, and rested for a couple of seconds.

Jules tried to stand, the weight of the chair causing her to lean heavily to the left. She turned with the momentum and fell backward against the wall. She could now use the wall to shimmy herself up. She had less than fifteen minutes left.

Jules rested when her right leg was fully extended, and then she leaped and extended her right leg so that all her weight would be on the left leg of the chair. The chair leg broke away, but she wasn't free of it, yet. She sat against the bed and rested again. Blood trickled from her forehead and left foot that had taken a beating. Her next trick was going to hurt even more so.

Now or never, she thought.

Jules stood on the bed, and faced a thick, white bear rug only three feet away. *Here goes nothing.* She bounced once on the bed, and threw her body into a three-quarter flip onto the bear rug. The impact shattered the seat from the back frame, but her arms were still tied to the rear styles. It also knocked the wind out of her when her elbows jammed into her stomach. She had taken harder falls off the balance beam. Her hands weren't free, but she could maneuver her arms that were still attached to the chair backing.

With her adrenalin on full rush, Jules walked to the bedroom door, turned herself a bit, and opened it. She attempted to open the front door in the same manner, but a deadbolt, placed high on the door, was out of her reach.

"Damn it—"

Jules pushed her arms as far out as the chair backing would allow her, and flung her arms up over her head and into a reverse dislocate. *Nothing new, I've thrown tighter dislocates on the uneven bars.*

247

With her arms in front of her, she smashed what was left of the chair backing on a nightstand until it shattered. Jules saw the blood dripping from her forehead, cheeks, and arms in a mirror. She grabbed the small plastic beeping device and her Glock, and then ran to the front door. She threw the deadbolt open, and walked into the open elevator.

The woman at the concierge desk saw blood pouring off of Jules. "Are you alright dear," she said, looking at the blinking device in Jules' hand.

"No, I'm in pain. May I borrow your phone?" Jules saw a pair of scissors sitting in a cup with some pens. She grabbed the scissors and snipped the friendship bracelet from her wrist. It fell to the floor as the woman handed her a cell phone. Jules saw the scared look on the woman's face. "It's some sort of bomb, and there's less than two minutes before it goes off. Make an announcement to clear the pool area and beach."

Jules hit the fire alarm by the rear door, and dialed Jacks R-CAT as she ran toward the pool area.

Fifty-five seconds.

Jack answered on the first ring. "Mameli."

"Jack, it's Jules.

"Where are you?"

Fifty seconds.

"I'm at the Seabreeze III. It was Bryce, Jack. I'm okay, but Big John is—"

"He's with me," Jack said. "We're on the way."

"Jack, Bryce left a half hour ago. She had some sort of bomb rigged to blow upstairs in her suite. It could be a small EMP, but I doubt it."

"Stay put Jules, Roy and BADDAY are on to her as we speak."

"I have the bomb in my hand, and It's going to blow in—twenty seconds." Jules dropped the phone and ran into the breaking waves. She wind milled her right arm a couple of times heaving the device, and then dove into a wave.

Three

Two

The explosion sent a rippling effect through the gulf and created waves almost two feet high in each direction. The impact of the force tumbled Jules backward onto the shore. Pieces of plastic fell harmlessly from the sky—the powerful gulf waters hindering any deathly impact. Dazed, she sauntered back up the beach and picked up the phone—it was still active.

"Jack?"

"Jules, what the—"

"It wasn't an EMP, but the explosion would have destroyed the penthouse of the hotel. Jack—the bitch tried to kill me."

"I'm coming—"

GENE HILGREEN

29

Seabreeze III Resort
Thursday April 11th

Jack pushed his way past the valet welcoming a throng of inebriated revelers returning to the resort well into the witching hour. He spotted Jules immediately. She was clad in a beach towel wrapped around her black bodysuit, and was propped up on a couch with a bloody towel wrapped around her head.

"Jules," he said, as he bumped into a porter pushing a luggage rack, causing the bags to fall to the floor only to block the hotel's revolving door.

Jules jumped up when she heard her name. The towel fell to the floor along with ice cubes that were numbing the bump on her head. "Where's Big John?" she asked with worry edging her voice.

Jack looked toward the front door and saw Big John helping a valet and porter restack the turned over luggage. He turned back toward Jules and pointed his thumb over his shoulder. "Right behind me . . . kinda."

Jules jumped into Jacks arms, and gave him a bear hug. Jack grabbed her by the hips and put her down on the floor. "You got some major explaining to do."

"Fine," she said, and ran toward Big John who put his hands out before she could leap onto him. "I thought you were gone," she said with tears in her eyes.

"Close," he said, and showed Jules his dog tags with the hole in it. "These babies saved my life."

"Do you need to see a doctor?" Jack asked.

"No. I'm okay. Let's get out of here. We have to find Bryce."

"You're going home young lady." Jack tossed the Tahoe keys to Big John. "You drive. I gotta call Anna."

Anna answered on the second ring. "Did you find her?"

"I got her. She was at the Seabreeze III Resort."

"Vat!"

"Bryce had captured her and there was a—" Jack stopped when Jules smacked him in the arm. He crunched his face at Jules and continued, "She's fine."

"I'm an hour out of Brownsville/SPI," Anna said. "Come get me with the Hughes . . . and bring Jules along."

"Roger that," Jack said. "You want to talk to her?"

"No. I *vant* to see her face . . . when she lies to me."

"Roy is searching the satellite feeds and resort video searching for Bryce's current whereabouts."

"Jack, Bryce was working on the EMP weapons project," Jules interjected. "I'm afraid she is going to take out the jet bringing in Russell and Davenport."

Jack gave Jules a 'shut the hell up' stare. "Relax Anna. We'll find her."

"Buck is *vith* me."

"Good," Jack said. "Put him on the phone. I'll meet you at the hanger."

An obnoxious buzz signaling an incoming hotel call woke Bryce who had fallen asleep in a club chair. As she reached for the phone, she noted the flashing red light informing her that she had messages. The LED clock on the phone blinked 7:36. She pulled back the curtain a few inches and answered the phone—morning sunlight creaked into the room.

"Hello?"

"Bryce, I've called you three times already," Kala said. "Are you alright?"

"Yes. Yes."

"From your message I thought it was urgent."

"It is, Kala. I need your help to get out of the country."

"What is it?"

"How soon can you get back from Las Lenas?"

"Actually, I'm in Cancun—skiing sucked. Bryce, are you in trouble?"

"Yes. Kala, I'm being framed for something I didn't do."

"I'm leaving now. You owe me Bryce. I'll be in Brownsville by two this afternoon."

"Thank you Kala. I owe you big time. Call me when you land and I'll tell you where to meet me." Bryce hung up and pulled the jammer from her bag on the table. "Thanks, Jules. So far—so good."

With this beauty, she thought, *I have some time.*

Although she preferred to work from the comforts of her home office on most days—Anna's office at the research center gave her access to technology and equipment found nowhere else on earth. The glass walls of the nanotechnology research laboratory that sat between her and Roy's office were black which told her Roy had initiated the SCIF mode. Something was going on that Roy didn't want anyone else to see. And only core members of The Corporation had access to the room.

Still steaming about the bomb that almost took Jules' life, Anna stood wearily before the security panel. She needed more sleep than the three hours that were given her. BADDAY acknowledged Anna and the door slid open. Jules impatiently pushed past Anna, and was quickly followed by Buck, Jack, and Big John.

Roy, Emma, and Jai stood surrounding a virtual, 3D holographic object, which was suspended in mid air. Emma touched one of the nanoparticles, and it detached from the main object to move out into its own rotating axis so the viewers could see the components in close detail as it revolved. Anna, Buck, and Jules joined the scientists while Jack and Big John grabbed seats and watched.

Emma turned toward the group. "Do you see what's missing?" She thought she knew.

Roy, Jai, and Jules shook their heads. Anna reached into the rotating sphere of nanoparticles, and zoomed out the outer covering of the core. "BADDAY, identify the particles and the core."

A list of meta-materials of the core and shield were displayed in a separate holograph. "There are no zero-valent ferrous nanoparticles in the shield." Anna walked away from the group. "We can't deactivate the nanobots remotely—we have to secure and destroy them manually."

Anna's R-CAT buzzed and a message scrolled across the screen. "The Russell's and Davenport's are at the security gate," she announced. "Buck and I will meet with them and make arrangements. Pack up the gear we will need for the EMP and let's meet back at the house at two p.m." Anna and Buck started to leave when Anna suddenly turned around. She caught Jules' attention by glaring unwaveringly at the girl. "Jack, please keep an eye on the *vanderer.*"

Feeling a little like a scolded child, Jules returned, "Do you want me to come with you?" Jules immediately regretted the question and found it strange that her voice sounded like an eleven-year-old's. She breathed out an audible breath of relief when she heard Anna's reply.

"No, that *von't* be necessary. Besides, you can help Roy set up your new R-CAT."

Kala had previously decided to cut her vacation short and head back to the island before getting the SOS from Bryce. Kala knew how Bryce ticked. Something didn't smell right to her, and she didn't get where she was by being played the fool. A quick trip to her penthouse was in order before she met up with Bryce.

When she walked out of the elevator into her suite, she tripped over a leg from her Queen Victorian chair—a very expensive piece, that was shattered and strewn about the room. Her living room looked like a war zone. Through the window overlooking the beach—she saw the pool and an area of beach roped off. SPIPD were combing the area with people in Hazmat suits.

More of Bryce's handiwork?

Kala passed through the dining room and into her master suite. On her dresser sat four bald heads—her wigs were missing. The French doors to her walk-in-closet were wide open, and outfits were strewn about—as if a fashion show used her room for changeovers. She noted that most of her favorite bodysuits were missing.

She pulled a book from the ornate bookcase—that also held a wide screen TV and entertainment system, and passed it across one of the columns. She heard the click of the magnet releasing the first lock. Next she pulled out a disguised shelf on the right side of the column. The shelf was also released by the powerful magnet in the book. She stopped on the third click, turned the knob, and pushed the shelf back into place. The column door popped open.

Inside the six by fourteen inch by six feet high hidden compartment hung an assortment of hand guns, and an AR15. She pulled out one of three center drawers that held visas, documents, and several throwaway cell phones. The other two drawers held priceless necklaces, rings, and earrings. She placed her travel etui in the middle drawer. The bottom of the compartment held four stacks of one-hundred dollar bills—banded into $100,000.00 bundles. There were twenty bundles the last time she looked, and a quick count confirmed that she still had two million in mad money. Kala took out two of the burner phones, the light weight Heckler & Koch USP 9mm pistol, and a fifteen round magazine.

Kala glanced around her bedroom looking for other missing objects; some of her favorite necklaces were also missing. Her anger echoed through the room when she smacked home the magazine and chambered a round. She set the safety switch on, and tucked the gun in the waist band at the small of her back. Not sure how to play Bryce just yet, she left her penthouse.

A nice high speed joy ride would give her time to think. At a quarter to two she called Bryce on one of the burner phones as she swung her black Porsche Turbo south onto Padre Boulevard.

Bryce let the phone ring four times, there was no caller ID. "Hello," she said.

"Bryce, its Kala . . . got in a little earlier than I thought. Where are you?"

"Damn, Kala you scared me to death. I'm at the Los Fresnos Inn. It's just north—"

"I know exactly where it is." Kala said, cutting Bryce off. "I'll be there in ten minutes—meet me in the lobby."

30

Anna's Island
Thursday June 11th

Anna angrily shoved herself away from the conference table and rose out of her chair. She walked to the large floor length window overlooking the bay. The tranquil waters of Laguna Madre did nothing to extinguish her ire. Hands on hips and with fire in her eyes, she turned back to the table where most of the core members of the Corporation sat.

Buck took a sip from his bottle of Corona, and then put it down. The assembled could visibly see how mad he was. Slapping his hands on the table, he stood up. He squeezed his fists together so tightly, his knuckles began to turn white.

"Sit! I'm not done talking yet." Anna ordered.

"Who died and made you God," Buck said, his voice taut. He looked straight at Anna's eyes, and they pleaded with him. He saw weakness there; a panicked grandmother, a deep instinctual hurting that someone dared to harm one of her family. He was shocked by her reaction, and it brought up his own panicked feelings to the surface. Relaxing his posture, he returned to his seat.

"Nobody died," Jules blurted out. "And by the way, Anna is God, Grandpa Buck."

Big John turned toward Jack and winked. "Told ya."Jack put his hands up in surrender, as did Buck and Roy. Emma's face fell, her eyes turned toward the table. Anna was her cousin and mentor, too—she kind of agreed with Jules.

"That's enough out of you two," Anna said, trying to be serious, but a slight smile made its way out. "This is a serious accusation, and the research center's reputation— my dream—is at stake."

"Anna's right," said Char, her voice emanating from the gadget at the center of the table. "I made Chief Smith an offer he couldn't refuse, and thanks to Jules, he's giving us forty-eight hours before he talks to the press. After that, he can't promise anything. The media is pushing for answers. People heard the explosion. They're talking, and they want answers."

"What about Russell and Davenport," Jack said. "Over at the coroner's office, they were jawing left and right about legal action."

"Buck and I talked to them at the dormitory while they were gathering their daughters' belongings. They know the center had nothing to do *with* it, and they are big donors to the program." Anna sat back down, turned to Jules and asked, "*Vat* I'd really like to know is how you ended up at the Seabreeze?"

Jules stood, and all eyes turned to her. "I wasn't completely honest. I have been following Dr. Kellogg."

"You promised to back off," Anna said. "I trusted you."

"Sorry Anna, but I've been doing some research on my own, and—"

"How?" asked Roy. "I've been monitoring you on BADDAY for the past two weeks."

Jules watched as Buck and Jack turned toward Big John. "It's not his fault. I approached Greg."

"What?" Jack asked in surprise.

"Okay, he caught me kind of breaking into his place, bought my story, and gave me search access."

"Great," Char said. "So Snowdan and the CIA know what's going on."

Jules giggled.

"What's so funny," Buck said. "You know you can't trust the CIA."

"Wow! I assumed you guys all thought I was smarter than that," Jules said. "I found the CIA's hidden folder on his system for the new satellites, and downloaded the access codes and programs to my laptop." Jules thumbed her chest. "Mind you, they didn't work. I had to fix them—"

Roy and Buck beamed. Anna's frown turned to a half smile.

"Jules gave me the programs a couple of days ago," Roy said. He paused a moment and then continued. "Sorry, but I never had the chance to look at them."

Jules came to Roy's rescue. "The satellites, have been storing data for the past four weeks, so I accessed it. They've been spying on SPI twenty-four-seven." Jules handed Roy a disc. "It's all on there. I was going to give it to you next week."

Anna started to rise, but then changed her mind. Tears began to form in her eyes. "Jules, honey. . . I love you, but your recklessness is scaring me." Anna paused to wipe away her tears. "I promised your mother that I *vould vatch* you."

Jules sat down and hugged Anna. "I love you, too." She said. She then stood and walked toward the window looking out on Laguna Madre Bay. "Looks like we're going to have another beautiful sunset today."

Buck stood, hands planted on the table, his jaw sawing. "Jules, damn it, this isn't cute anymore."

Jules turned from the window and saw that everyone was staring at her. "Maybe you all haven't noticed," She shifted her eyes toward Big John and winked, "but I'm a big girl now and can take care of myself."

"You're still a minor, damn it." Buck said.

Anna patted his arm. "Sit down, Buck. Let her continue. Now please tell us what you've found?"

"Dr. Kellogg never left the island—"

Still not knowing what to expect, Kala left all avenues open as she walked into the foyer of the Los Fresnos Inn. She stopped dead in her tracks when she saw her spitting image sitting on a settee. She walked straight toward Bryce who could have passed for her twin. "Care to explain?"

"Not here, Kala," Bryce said as she hugged her. "Let's go to my room."

Kala accepted Bryce's hand, but not without sending a frown of annoyance to her friend. As they walked hand-in-hand to Bryce's room, Kala stopped. "You do have something to drink?"

"I have tequila," Bryce offered, but I can call room service.

"Tequila will be fine."

After gaining entry to the room, Bryce filled two rocks glasses halfway and handed one to Kala. "I'm in a deep jam . . . remember when I told you about my father?"

"Don't tell me you have something to do with those dead girls." Kala downed her drink, and refilled her glass.

She pointed the bottle toward Bryce, who nodded, and Kala moved to fill hers, too.

"Yes," she said, and took a long sip from the glass.

"Do tell—please."

Bryce sat on the bed. "The girls were the daughters of the men responsible for my father's suicide. I wanted to hurt them bad—everything just kind of fell into place. Remember the pervert I was telling you about?"

Kala nodded and shook her glass, motioning Bryce to continue.

"I started following him after I caught him eyeing the two girls. He pretty much left them for dead after he had his way with them. I just finished his job for him, making sure the evidence pointed the cops right to him. But—"

Kala had heard enough. "Why do you look like my twin sister?"

"I was getting to that. I—"

"Get to it now."

"The darling of the research center Jules Spenser started snooping around." Bryce got up and poured herself another drink. "Kala, I really like this kid, but she was on to me. She even went to the jail to talk to the guy who was arrested."

"Tell me more about him." Kala asked, as she filled up her glass with some ice and water. "What was his name again?"

"Tony Labarbera. He works for the cleaning company that takes care of the research center."

"I know him," Kala said. "He tried to pour his charm on me several times, but I blew him off. He goes for the money, but I'm sure he likes his girls young and simpleminded."

"That's the point. He started chasing Jules, and I let my guard down. Jules started following him and it led to me. Sorry, Kala. That's when I sort of became you."

"What?"

"When I started following him, I began wearing your wigs and outfits. I just wanted to have some fun. A new wardrobe, a little makeup, and bam! I changed from Bryce the nerd into Kala the hot, sexy world traveler."

"So what happened?"

"Jules must have followed me to the Seabreeze, where I caught her snooping around."

"And?"

Bryce knew the explosive device would wreak havoc in the penthouse suite, and keep the local cops busy. She also hoped that Jules was smart enough to protect herself from fall out. But if she didn't—Bryce could live with that.

"I shot her bodyguard and kidnapped her. She's fine. I'll make a call when I'm safely out of the country."

"Where is—" Kala stopped mid sentence. She didn't want Bryce to know that she had already seen the wreckage at her penthouse, and knew that Jules had escaped. "What are your plans?" she asked instead. "I have money back at my suite—you're welcome to it."

"I'll be fine Kala. I just need to get out of the country."

"Okay then. What's your plan?"

31

Anna's Island
Thursday April 11th

Jules had everyone's attention as she played back the first video sequence she had bookmarked earlier. "Watch this," she said, and broke the video into two segments. "Here's Kala leaving from Brownsville/SPI International on her private jet." Jules pointed to the other screen. "Now here's Kala, which BADDAY shows as a ninety percent match, leaving the Seabreeze two hours later."

"How do we know that it's not Kala?" Buck asked.

"Grandpa," Jules began. Giggles erupted from Big John and Jack until they were met with Buck's scowl at which time they ceased immediately. "I verified Kala

267

GENE HILGREEN

landed in Las Lenas, and she immediately went shopping with her Black American Express." She added air quotes as she announced the credit card company.

"Who taught you how to do that?" Buck asked.

Jules choked as she tee-heed so hard that tears came to her eyes. "You're kidding right?" she said between gasps. "Look at the company I keep."

"The apple doesn't fall far from the tree," Jack said, which was promptly answered with a smack from Anna. "The little girl is . . . *how do you say it* . . . all *growed* up."

Anna smiled.

Jules burst out laughing.

"Jules, get serious," Anna said. "Please continue your presentation."

"Sorry," she said, as Big John tossed her a bandana to wipe away her tears. She caught it and asked. "Is it clean?"

Big John winked.

"Jules!" said Anna.

"Okay! Here's Kala returning to the Seabreeze an hour after leaving." Jules gazed at her audience. "Anyone care to know what this other Kala did for that hour?"

"Jules!" said the voice emanating from the triangular device in the center of the conference table.

"Sorry, Madame President."

"It's Char, Jules."

"She was at the International Bank of Commerce SPI, and thanks to one of the programs I borrowed from Greg the Spook. I learned that she cleared her account and

268

transferred it to a bank in the Caymans. The trace ended there."

"Jules, I thought you wanted to be a Quantum Physicist," Char said.

"I do," Jules replied. "But I also want to be a spy like Buck, Jack, and Anna."

"That's not funny Jules," Anna said. "And if I have anything to say, your sleuthing days are over."

"Shall I continue?" Jules asked.

"Please do," Anna said.

Jules restarted the video at the next bookmark. "Here is Bryce leaving the Seabreeze as herself." Jules fast forward the video to show Bryce entering Brownsville SPI International. "I hacked into the NTSB database—"

"How? Buck asked. "Never mind . . . continue please."

"—and verified that Bryce was on her way to New York's, LaGuardia airport. She had a three hour layover at George Bush Intercontinental Airport in Houston." Jules jumped the video feed to her next bookmark. "Bryce never boarded the plane to New York. The flight was for show. Here is the Kala look-alike exiting Brownsville SPI Intercontinental. I verified again with NTSB and the flight from Houston was for Kala Kellingworth."

Anna stood and marched toward her glass wall. She knew the view of the tranquil bay would calm her fury somewhat, at least to the point of control. "Damn her. I fell for her story."

"Anna, we all did," Jules said.

"I don't get fooled easily," Anna replied.

"Do we know where she is?" Char asked.

Roy stood up. His facial expression was one of embarrassment and concern. "BADDAY lost her, and I don't know how."

"Roy, it's not your or BADDAY's fault," Jules said.

Roy raised his head and looked at Jules. "The missing jammer?"

"Yes," Jules said, and began to cry. "Sorry everyone, but I saw it on the Tiki Bar and took it. I wanted to see what made it tick. I lost it the night that Bryce grabbed me. She must have it."

"I know what to do," Roy said. "But I'm going to need some help. Emma are you coming?"

Roy, Emma, and Jai left the table.

"Wait," said Jules. "I want to help. It's my fault."

"No," Anna said. "*Ve* are not done talking."

"Let her go," Buck said. "I want to see this gadget myself."

"Fine. Go then. I need to tend to Russell and Davenport anyway," Anna said. "Char, I'll call you when we locate Bryce."

"Big John and I are coming with you," Jack said. "We'll get their luggage loaded in the Hughes.

Kala listened to Bryce's plans for the next hour while they ate a late lunch in the hotel's restaurant. Her idea of flying out of General Lucio Blanco International Airport in Reynosa, TAMPS, Mexico held some merit, but Kala thought she could sneak her into Brownsville SPI International where her private jet sat in a private hanger.

"Okay, let me see if I got this straight," Kala said. "I'm going to race down Route 77 to Route 83—draw attention to myself, and then take Route 491 or Route 281 to the border."

"Yes, and I will cross the border at one of the rinky-dink crossings, and we'll meet up on Mexico Route 2—the Autopista Matamoros-Reynosa."

"Why not?" Kala said. "I've wanted to open up the Porsche ever since I got it. When do we go?"

"At sundown."

"Any luck yet?" Anna asked, as she entered the Nanoscience lab.

Emma shook her head. "BADDAY has located Kala Kellingworth, but not Bryce."

Roy stood in front of two large flat screen monitors. One monitor had a thermal GPS view of the Los Fresnos Inn. The other with a thermal IPS view of the room Kala was identified in. He pointed to the thermal GPS view of the parking lot. "We have identified that Porsche as belonging to Kala Kellingworth. Roy pointed at the

271

thermal IPS view. "This is Kala Kellingworth—it's a one-hundred-percent match. While we can't identify this other heat mass, my gut tells me it's Bryce. She's either shielded or has a better jammer then we do."

"It's getting late," Anna said. "Jack and Big John have already left for Brennan Farm with Russell, Davenport, and a security detail."

"We need more time," Roy said.

Anna walked toward the exit. "Time *ve* don't have."

"Where are you going?" Buck asked."

"The Fresnos Inn."

"No," Buck said. "You stay here with them. I'll go. Jules you're with me."

Buck we talked about this," Anna said.

"Listen. From everything I heard, Jules knows Bryce better than anyone." Buck gave a pat to his holstered Glock. "You armed, Jules?"

Jules turned to show Buck her Glock-26 nestled securely in her waist holster.

"Good. Let's go."

"Please be careful," Anna said to deaf ears as Buck and Jules pushed through the doors.

Jules pressed the APP to fire up the Ferrari as they exited the research center.

"Don't even think about it," Buck said, as he jingled the keys. "I'm driving. You're my eyes and ears."

32

The Chase
Thursday April 11th

The Ferrari speedometer sat at forty kilometers per hour for the whole ride through Port Isabel, Laguna Heights, and into Los Fresnos—a fraction less, Buck had calculated than the posted thirty miles-per-hour speed limit.

"Come on Buck," Jules said. "You're killing me here. Give this baby a little gas."

"Jules, I told you they don't mess around in these towns. Speeding tickets pay the bills. Plus they lock you up for a couple of hours just to mess with you."

"Is that experience talking?"

Buck tilted his head in a mocking manner, shifted his eyes toward Jules, and winked. "You bet."

A chirp from the inboard GPS system caught Jules's attention. "Buck, the Porsche is leaving the hotel. Step on it!"

Buck pressed the pedal to the floor. The Ferrari sped through the night and the road signs became a blur. The Ferrari seemed to beg for more as it chirped off their speed as the car quickly accelerated to a dangerous velocity.

Buck stole a glance at Jules while reaching into his pocket for his *get out of jail free card*, the business card of an old friend. Jules' hand rubbed the baby Glock tucked in her waistband—her face tight and eager.

Damn, he thought, *she likes this too much. She's gonna follow in my footsteps.*

"How's school?" he asked to break the tension. "You look lost in thought."

"School's fine," she replied. "I'm not lost or trying to find myself, are you?"

"Jules...cut the shit."

"I know what I want to do, and, for your information, I can do both—faster, Grandpa."

She's pissed, thought Buck. *She called me Grandpa.*

Now, staring into her face, he saw it, too. She needed the same kind of daily adrenaline rush that he did. She needed a gun on her hip and somebody to hunt. "Honey. I carry the weight of the world on my shoulder. I protect America. I only have two hands, but I'm trained for this. And that's fine by me."

"Well shit happens," Jules said. "And it effects more than the good old U.S. of A. You ought to open your eyes to that fact sometime."

Buck had never heard Jules curse before, and needed to reel her in. "Life is not a game you play on your computer—this is real."

Jules harrumphed, and laid her head back into the cushions of the headrest. "Well. Wake me up when it's over."

The exit sign for the town of Mercedes came and went. They were gaining on the Porsche, but the exit they passed was Route 491, and led to U.S. Route 281—known to locals as Military Highway. It ran along the Rio Grande River that separated the U.S. from Mexico. Buck instinctively knew nothing good was going to come of this.

Buck eased the Ferrari down and smacked Jules in the arm. "You want in? You'd better snap out of that funk you're in." He punched the console for effect. "You gotta get over your demons. Wake up honey! You have to deal with everyone, including men your own age."

"I'm trying, Buck!"

Buck pulled his eyes from the road for a second and smacked Jules again—with love this time." Well search harder, this is real, damn it."

"I didn't know I was this far gone until now. I was finding myself. Anna's right—I'm messed up."

"You're not messed up honey. You were lost."

"Not anymore. Faster."

275

Buck turned his eyes back to the road, and with a smile on his face, firmly planted his foot on the accelerator. "Good. We'll talk more about this later," he said, and then handed her a business card and ordered, "Get that guy on the phone."

Jules read the card. "Who the hell is Octavia Perez?"

"An old friend, so to speak, told me I'm not in Colorado anymore when he gave me my tenth speeding ticket." A mischievous smile spread across his face. "Said we should have lunch some day and talk. I think now is as good a time as any."

Confused, Jules punched the number into the screen on the dashboard phone system.

An angry voice answered. "It's eight o'clock. Someone better be dying."

"Octavia, it's Buck—"

"Buck Axele Davidssen?" Chief of Police Perez asked. "What can I do for my favorite Coloradan?"

"Got a situation here. I'm chasing a Porsche 911 through your lovely jurisdiction. The perp is suspected of murder."

"What, may I ask, are you driving?"

Buck let out a hearty laugh. "Something you can't catch. It'll be like the old days. You can bring the ticket to my place of work."

"Not funny, Buck. Why am I hearing this from you, and not from my scanner?"

"Blackout came from the top," Buck explained. "I'm calling in favors for my boss."

Octavia knew Buck had an unusual job with the government; he had flashed every badge imaginable to get out of tickets. "Which boss?" he asked, a slight chuckle in his voice.

"Charlotte."

"The president?" This time his voice was serious. "Heard that you made her an honest woman. That so?"

Jules let out her first laugh of the night.

"Who's that with you?"

"My granddaughter, Jules," Buck answered, and put a hand to his lips to shush her.

"Ah, the champion gymnast," Octavia said. "What do you need from me?"

"Road blocks both ways on Military Highway at Routes 1015, 493 and 281 south." Pausing, Buck weighed in on filling the police chief with more details. Then deciding, he simply continued with, "We believe the perp is headed for General Lucio Blanco Airport in Reynosa, Mexico."

"Got a name?"

"Need to know," Buck said.

"*Pendejo!*"

"Been called worse. We need her alive."

"Now we're getting somewhere. You owe me Buck. Consider it done."

Chief Perez put out a stop and detain order for the Porsche, no questioned asked. He was to be called immediately when the vehicle was spotted. Road blocks were set up on Route 281 running north and south, and Military Highway—oddly also labeled Route 281—running east and west. Another road block was set up on Route 493 and 1015 just before the border. All three routes led to the Autopista Matamoros-Reynosa Highway, which led directly to the General Lucio Blanco International Airport. Chief Perez believed that one of the latter two routes would be chosen because of the lax security at those border points. He headed to Route 1015—easily the most lax of them all.

Jules was toying with the GPS view, zooming the display screen in and out. "Buck. Something doesn't seem right," she said.

"What makes you say that?"

"I was thinking about Dr. Russell and Dr. Davenport. What airport are they leaving from?"

"Brennan's Farm," Buck answered, a quizzical sound to his voice. "It's a private airfield just south of Los Fresnos and Highway 100. Why do you ask?"

"I think we got hoodwinked again. Something just doesn't feel right."

Jules pushed the thermal GPS button on the Ferrari dashboard system. "BADDAY, locate Kala Kellingworth and Dr. Bryce Kellogg."

A few seconds later, two dots appeared on the screen. One dot was moving west on Military Highway just past Progreso, Texas, about five miles away from Route 493. The other dot sat stationary on Old Alice Road—two miles south of Route 100 in Los Fresnos.

"One-hundred percent match for Kala Kellingworth heading west on Military Highway," said the computerized voice of BADDAY. "Eight-six percent match for Kala Kellingworth on Old Alice Road."

"What about Dr. Bryce Kellogg?" Jules asked tensely.

"Dr. Bryce Kellogg not found, tracker disabled."

"Shit."

"What?" Buck asked.

"Turn around. That has to be Bryce on Old Alice Road."

Buck slammed on the breaks and cut across the center divider on Route 83—fishtailing through the turn. Once the Ferrari was righted, he floored it. "Call Chief Perez," Buck ordered. "Tell him to head for Route 493."

GENE HILGREEN

33

Old Alice Road - Los Fresnos, Texas
Thursday night April 11th

Bryce heard the alert over her police scanner. She was less than a quarter-mile from Brennan's Farm Airport, and could see the activity through the high-powered scope attached to her rocket launcher. She took a big chance exiting the shielded protection of the Porsche, and was aware that she could be picked up by BADDAY's GPS system, but she couldn't see the jet from the car.

Bryce lowered the launcher and retreated to her car. She had bought the black, Porsche 911 GT3 RS Turbo earlier in the week with Kala's American Express Centurion Card—also known as the *black card*. She called Kala on a burner phone.

"Bryce," Kala answered. "What the hell is going on? I thought you said this would be a piece of cake—there're cop cars chasing me."

"Relax, Kala, and don't do anything stupid. Just make it across the border. I will meet you there as soon as I am done."

"Fine. Hurry."

Bryce disconnected the call, looked into the rearview mirror, and winked. "Hello Kala Kellingworth," she said. She pushed the ignition button, and put the Porsche in gear. She had seen all she needed to.

A few minutes earlier, Jack Mameli had dropped off Russell and Davenport. The transport that carried the caskets for Sandy and Mary Francis' bodies had just arrived. Bryce had watched as the dead girls' luggage was loaded onto the jet. Her judgment was severely impaired by anger. Originally, she had planned to blow the jet out of the sky upon takeoff.

She had several options available, providing Kala's identity could carry her through successfully. She had smuggled a laptop and some nanobots into one of the girls' suitcases. The laptop was programmed to activate the nanobots one hour after takeoff. By her calculations, the nanobots would then eat through the Jet's metal body within twenty-two minutes. Whatever was leftover, including Doctors Russell and Davenport would fall from the sky in a fiery wreck. By that time, she would be winging somewhere over the Atlantic Ocean.

The situation had grown more complicated but not unmanageable. Since her father's suicide, Bryce always had a Unitarian outlook about friends: don't use anyone you're not willing to lose.

There would be collateral damage, of which Kala Kellingworth would be a part of. Bryce decided she could live with that, and would assume Kala's identity for now. She had already moved Kala's bank account from the International Bank of Commerce SPI to an account in the Cayman Islands. Within a week, Bryce would have a completely new identity, and plenty of money to renew her research.

Bryce harbored no hatred for Jules. Some annoyance, of course, but it was tempered by admiration. The protégée child was every bit as good as her growing reputation. Now Bryce hoped to touch something vital within Jules. Any major artery would do.

Bryce took side roads to Brownsville South Padre Island International Airport. She never saw the Ferrari when it turned down Old Alice Road. She was too busy phoning Kala for the last time.

"Bryce," Kala answered. "Where are you? I'm scared. There's a road block just ahead of me on Route 493 before the border."

"Relax, Kala. Everything will be alright. I'll be there in ten minutes. Pull off to the side of the road and wait for me."

Kala eased her Porsche onto the gravel at the road's edge and turned off the engine. She nervously looked in her rearview mirror to see if anyone had been following her. Even though no other cars drove by, she felt scared to death. She could feel her heart thundering in her chest. She quickly thought through the different scenarios which had led to her current predicament, and her mind churned for an answer as to how she might safely extricate herself from the mess.

Bryce disconnected the call, casually picked up a remote from the seat beside her, and after a few moments of thought, pushed a button on the remote. "Goodbye, Kala."

A minute later an explosion ripped through Kala's car, lifting it off the ground and blowing pieces of metal for two-hundred feet in every direction.

The Ferrari's integrated phone system rang. "Jules here."

"It's Octavia Perez, is Buck still with you?"

"Yes," Buck said. "I'm here. What do you got?"

"Remember that Porsche we were chasing? Well it just exploded in a ball of flames off Route 493. Buck, there's nothing left but pieces."

"The driver?" Buck asked.

"Nothing. Nothing but little pieces of scrap scattered everywhere. I don't think forensics will even be able to ID the driver, it's that bad."

"Shit. Give me half an hour. I have another situation at Brennan's Farm."

"What?"

"A jet might be next."

"Buck. We gotta talk. I liked it better when you moved back to Colorado."

"Love you, too, Octavia."

"Buck, stay where you are. My men can handle this. I'm on my way."

"Later," Buck said, and hit the button to disconnect.

Jack turned as the Ferrari barreled down the runway, power slid, and came to a stop no more than twenty feet from the jet. Buck and Jules jumped out of the car and ran straight toward him.

"What's wrong?" Jack asked. Buck could detect a slight ruffle in the man's usually calm and collected tone of voice.

"Get everyone off the jet. Now!" Buck ordered. "The luggage, too."

"What's going on, Buck?"

"We believe Bryce is planning to take out the jet. I just got a call from Chief Perez, the Porsche we were chasing exploded. Bryce is covering all of her bases."

"You heard the man," Jack said to the security detail. "Get everything off this jet!"

Buck phoned Anna to fill her in. She was at the research center reviewing all the projects Bryce had been working on, and heard all of the conversation that had taken place in the Ferrari. It was, after all, her car, and the phone system was linked to her R-CAT.

"I'm sending a group of scientists to Brennan's as we speak," she said. "How is Jules?"

Buck looked toward Jules and got a face. "She's fine. A little pissed, but fine."

"Let me talk to her."

Buck handed the phone over to Jules. "It's Anna, and she's worried."

Jules took the phone. "I'm fine Anna, but please hurry. Bryce got away."

Twenty minutes later, Anna arrived at Brennan Farm with a team of scientists armed to the teeth with equipment. They scanned the jet, pilots, passengers, and the entire luggage after it had been removed from the jet. When the nanobots were identified, they were placed in a shielded compartment to be destroyed at a later date. The scientists followed Chief Perez back to the crash site to aid forensics with the search for DNA.

Meanwhile, Dr. Roy Singh and Jai were in his office at the research center trying everything they could to find Dr. Bryce Kellogg. He was joined by Buck, Jack, Anna, and Jules within the hour.

"Nothing," Roy said when the group pulled up chairs to his desk.

"She can change her identity," Anna said, "but she can't change her DNA. We will find her."

Jules stood up and walked over to a wall of windows. She saw Big John, Emma, and Greg riding in a golf cart, making their way across the bridge toward the research center. When she turned back to the group she noticed everyone's eyes were turned to her.

"*Vat* are you thinking, Jules?" Anna asked.

"I have some ideas," she answered. "I want this project."

Roy pushed a button which lowered some panels from the ceiling and covered the wall of glass. It was just a precaution, and he just wanted a pure SCIF.

BADDAY announced there were visitors outside his office. Roy acknowledged and allowed BADDAY to open the door. Big John, Greg, Emma, and Gunny entered, and took up seats as close to the main group as possible.

Jules smiled when she saw Big John. She walked over to the couch he was sitting on, and plopped down beside him.

Roy pressed the communication device on his desk, and the face of Charlotte Vice-Davidssen filled the flat screen monitors along the wall. She was in her private law office at Vice, Banker, and Vice in DC. It's not that she didn't trust the White House—she just trusted her office more.

"We're all here, Madam President," Roy said.

"Hello, all," she said. "Great job keeping this mess quiet. Dr. Kellogg is a brilliant woman, and from what

Roy tells me, she's an asset we don't want to lose. She will pay for her crimes, but as far as anyone is concerned, Tony Labarbera will take the rap for everything. Any questions?"

Jules stood up. "But Tony didn't kill those girls."

We don't know that for a fact," Char said. "And besides, Chief Smith has him on kidnapping, rape, and attempted murder. Tony will spend a long time in jail, which is where he belongs."

"I want in," Jules demanded.

"You are in, Jules," Char replied. "You are part of the inner core of The Corporation. Hell, one day you'll be running it, but for now you need to sit back and let the pros handle this situation."

DDHS Micky Livingston's face appeared next to Chars. "Jules, Char is right. You have a lot more training ahead of you. Not to mention, you already had a close call there."

Jules turned to sit back down, whispering "Say's you." She smiled at Big John who looked toward the ceiling. Jules followed his gaze and noticed the eye in the sky, realizing BADDAY had heard her, too. "Damn."

"Alright, now," said Char. She swirled a glass filled with her favorite scotch, and then took a sip before continuing. "I've signed a Presidential Finding treating Dr. Kellogg as a possible terrorist, and it goes no further than this group. The project is completely funded." She paused a moment to sip at her glass again. "Buck and Jack, it's a go. Find this woman."

"Dalwinnie?" Buck asked.

"The scotch of Gods." Char replied.

Buck chuckled at the reference. "On it honey," he said.

"If it's not too much trouble," Char said with a wink. "Could you stop in DC while you're on your way?"

Whitecloud and Priest filled the screen behind Char. "Yo. Semper Fi Cap'n," they said in tandem, and both raised their glasses.

"Tell me you two are drinking real scotch?"

"Only the best," said Whitecloud. "Macallan twenty-five."

"Ooh Rah," Buck said. "Give me and Jack a day or two to wrap this up."

"Just call me when you're wheels up," Char said, and cut off the connection.

GENE HILGREEN

34

Anna's Island
Friday April 12th

No one noticed the figure as it left the Porsche to blend into the night. Believing Bryce was up to no good, Kala had gotten out of the vehicle to run her bug detector over her phone and body. The friendship bracelet she was wearing beeped, indicating it was a GPS tracker. She ripped it off her wrist and threw it to the ground in disgust. She didn't feel safe sitting on the open road just a minute's drive away from a police road block, and decided it was too risky to use the Porsche that was probably on every policeman's *detain list* across the entire state by now.

She dialed a number on her cell phone in the hopes she could get picked up before she was detained by police forces. The blast wave from the explosion blew her to the ground, and she heard a whine buzz right beside her ear as a chunk of metal zipped passed her head and on further into the darkness in front of her.

She hid in a field, waiting to be picked up. A dark sedan rounded the corner of the road and slid to a stop. Kala quickly made her way to the car, and with a heavy breath of relief, wearily sat down onto the backseat.

"Where to, Ma'am?"

"Home, James," Kala said. "I've got some planning to do."

Buck had one more piece of business to attend to before he left for DC. He and Roy were seated around the oval conference table in Anna's office, digesting the resume of Dr. Jace Badaskar while Anna looked on. Anna had the pleasure of working with Jace at NASA years earlier. As an exchange student from Bandapor, India, Jace was assigned to Anna's Clinical Biochemistry team. Jace eventually received her PhD in Nanobiotechnology and specialized in structural DNA nanotechnology—the natural occurring structures and phenomena in biochemistry.

"Thought she would be a perfect fit here," Anna said.

"Call her in," Roy said.

Anna turned her eyes toward Buck. "*Vell?*"

"I'm okay with it," Buck said. "But you're not going to make me sit through your chat, too, are you?"

"No, but I want Jules, Jai, and Gunther here."

"Good. They're at the range with Jack. I'll send them over."

Buck opened the door to Anna's office and motioned Emma and Jace to enter. Emma, dressed in one of her bodysuits displaying an obscene amount of cleavage was not what caught Bucks attention. "Nice rack," he commented anyway.

What did catch his eye was the other young woman's colorful silk Salwar Kameez—a traditional Hindu garment—that did nothing to distract from her beauty. He looked back into the room at Roy and winked. "Have fun," he said.

Buck left and grabbed one of the golf carts from the garage and drove over the bridge. At the guard booth stood a black haired version of Anna arguing with the guard.

"May I help you?" Buck asked.

"Thank you Mr. Davidssen," the guard said. "This woman says she is—"

"Kala Kellingworth." The woman then offered her hand to Buck. "I'd like to speak with Dr. Semyonova."

"Mr. Davidssen," the guard said. "Dr. Semyonova told me no interruptions for the next hour."

"Thank you Jessy," Buck said. "I've got this. Give her a visitor's badge." Buck hit the icon on his R-CAT for Jack.

293

Several rings later, Jack answered. "What's up Cap'n?"

"Bring the kids and meet me at my beach house. I've got something you'll want to see."

Twenty minutes later, Jack along with Jules, Jai, and Gunther found Buck, Big John, and a knockout with long brown hair and piercing brown eyes sitting at a picnic table, drinking Coronas.

"Meet Kala Kellingworth," Buck said.

Jack had to hold Jules back as he offered his hand. "I'm Jack Mameli."

"Damn," Jules said, and offered her hand. "I'm Jules Spenser, and OMG."

"Pull up a seat, Jules," Buck said. "And put a zipper on it. Kala was just about to explain everything."

Several beers later, Buck and the gang had been hearing Bryce's life through the eyes of Kala, after which, Buck called Anna on a secure channel of his R-CAT.

"*Vat's* the matter?"

"I'm at my beach house with Kala Kellingworth."

"Who else is there?"

"The whole gang. Where do you want to meet?"

"Come here. Char *vill vant* to hear this, too."

After everyone had gathered at Anna's office, Kala retold the story to Char, Anna, and the other core members. Meanwhile, Buck and Roy worked on retrieving Kala's money from the Cayman account Bryce had set up. This wouldn't be the first time Buck had hacked into a Cayman account to retrieve ill-gotten gains. Jules ran searches through every flight database looking for booked flights in either Kala or Bryce's names. Jai, on the other hand, couldn't keep his eyes off of the beautiful twenty-six-year-old Jace.

"Hey," Jules said. "I have something here." All the eyes in the room turned toward her. Jules looked at Kala. "There's a Kala Kellingworth on a United Air flight to George Bush Intercontinental Airport in Houston out of Brownsville, connecting with British Air to London." Jules paused. "That flight was yesterday, and she wasn't on it."

"Jules," Char said. "I put Kala Kellingworth and Bryce Kellogg on the TSA's (Transportation Security Administration) no-fly list. She must have gotten spooked by the extra agents I asked for at the security check-in."

Jules looked back at the flight record. "This is weird," she said. "The flight out of Houston is for tomorrow."

Buck smiled. "She's not flying out of Brownsville. She's driving to Houston. Anybody know what kind of wheels she has?"

"Damn, I almost forgot," Kala said. "I got a call from American Express while I was in Las Lenas. A used 2018, black, Porsche 911 GT3 RS Turbo was purchased with my card. I figured it was Bryce and let it slide."

"Rich are we?" Jules said.

Before Kala could answer, Char chimed in. "Jules, her family's money makes my family look poor."

Kala smiled. "Thank you, Madam President." She said, and then turned toward Jules. "My father is a big contributor to Anna's program."

Char winked back from one of the wall monitors.

Buck ran a DMV search on Kala and the Porsche. He entered the serial numbers into the GPS tracking system. "BADDAY, find that Porsche." Buck opened the GPS program on one of the unused flat screen wall monitors, and watched as BADDAY began its search.

Where would you like your money transferred?" Roy said, looking at Kala. It was the first time he'd raised his eyes from his laptop since the meeting started.

"That was fast," Kala said, and wrote down a number to an offshore account. "Put it in here, if you can."

"No problem."

BADDAY had zoomed in on a black Porsche speeding north on Route 77 just north of Corpus Christi, Texas.

"Jack," Buck said. "Whatta you say we take the Hughes for a spin, and end this tonight."

Jules stood up as Jack started for the door. "I'm going, too."

Buck looked toward Anna and Char. Char nodded.

"Go," Anna said. "But we have to finish our talk when you get back."

Jules didn't wait, and was out the door ahead of Jack.

"Call you when we're wheels up," Buck said, and started for the door.

"Buck, I want her alive. She will never make it into the airport," Char said, and then added. "She's a brilliant physicist, and I have just the right team to fix her."

"I'll try."

True to her word, Char had every entrance to George Bush Intercontinental Airport guarded. Bryce surrendered to the secret service at the entrance on Will Clayton Parkway when her Porsche was blocked by several nondescript black Tahoe's. She was taken into custody and turned over to Buck at a private hanger—no questions asked.

Char had sent Whitecloud, Priest, and a crew of scientists to meet Buck, Jack, and Jules in Houston.

Bryce no longer had fire in her eyes as Buck and Jack secured her in one of The Corporation's private jets. In fact the only person spewing any fire in their eyes was Jules, who sat directly across from her for the short flight to Sardy Field in Aspen.

"Jules, I'm sorry—"

"Sorry nothing," Jules interrupted. "You're going to pay for this Bryce."

"They killed my father."

"And they will pay, too," Jules said. "Anna and Char insured me that they will look very closely into Russell and Davenport's involvement."

Jack sat down next to Bryce and gave her his death stare.

"Jules, Gunny is waiting for you," Buck said. "Your presence is requested back at the island. You're done here."

"But—"

"But nothing," Buck said. The muscles in his jaw twitching stopped Jules cold.

"Fine," she said, and looked past Buck. Gunny stood on the exit stairs flashing a thumb up.

"Come on kid," Gunny said. "You can fly us back."

Jules got up from the seat and started for the exit, but not before adding her two cents. "We're not done yet Bryce—not by a long shot."

"So be it," Bryce said.

Jules stomped down the aisle, but a smile spread across her face when Gunny handed her the keys to the Hughes.

"Thanks Gunny," Buck said. "See you in a couple of days."

"Semper Fi, Cap'n"

"Ooh rah," Buck replied.

EPILOGUE

With the sun looming over the horizon, the Laguna Madre bay appeared to burn with an array of colors from burnt orange to a deep purple. "Gunny, I have to get a picture of this," Jules pleaded.

Gunny snapped off a few pictures with his R-CAT, and then hit the icon on his phone for Anna.

While entertaining guests at the Tiki bar, Anna kept a watchful eye on the horizon for the Hughes and answered on the first ring. "I have you in sight. Tell Jules to loop around the island so I can snap a few pictures with the sunset."

"You read my mind," Gunny said.

As Jules looped around the island, she knew something was up when she noted the group of people

299

gathered at the Tiki bar. "Anna, get a picture with the sun setting behind us," Jules said.

"Okay, bring her in," Anna said, and disconnected the call.

Jules turned toward Gunny. "That's some interesting group assembled at the Tike bar," she said.

Gunny gave Jules a wink and a smile as she landed the Hughes.

The crowd at the Tiki Bar stood as Jules and Gunny approached.

"I guess I'm getting my talk." Jules said, noting that DDHS Micky Livingston and SPIPD Chief Smitty were among the group with Anna.

"You knew it was coming," Gunny said. "Just suck it up and take it like a big girl."

"Have a seat honey," Anna said. "It's time to set the rules straight."

Micky started, and explained the Department of Homeland Security's interest in the research center and why it was important for Jules to focus on her studies. Chief Smitty followed, and although it was agreed that she would still help out with his computer systems—her sleuthing days were over. Jules, however, had her fingers crossed behind her back the whole time while she agreed.

Anna closed the discussion, using access to the Ferrari and Hughes as collateral as she laid down the law. Roy and Emma added bits and pieces to the discussion, but Jules was barely listening at that point. She didn't want to lose the Ferrari and Hughes, and promised that her studies would come first, and her spare time would be spent in the gym.

With Bryce secured and confined at Angel's Landing under house arrest, the island returned to its normal peacefulness. Jules spent her mornings in class and her afternoons at the gym. Over the next couple of weeks Jules and Jai became closer, but that's where their relationship ended. Jai had eyes only for Dr. Jace Badaskar.

Jules, however, forgave Gunther for mauling her at Louie's, and the two began to spend their off-time together at the gun range and gym.

Jack constantly reminded Gunther that Jules was only seventeen—he also kept his fake ID. Gunther was permitted to have beers on Anna's island, but no more drinking at the clubs until he was twenty-one. He was still under probation per Jack—and no one messes with Jack.

The following Friday night, Buck walked into his beach house, and was met by utter silence.

"Did I miss something?" Buck asked as he closed the front door.

"No sir," Gunther replied.

"Everything is under control," Jack announced. "Jules and Gunther are taking the Hunter out."

"Kala and I are going, too," Big John added.

With his right index finger extended and his thumb cocked, Buck pointed at Gunther. Buck then turned to Jack. "We have to get back to Angel's Landing—troubles are brewing. Your call, we can leave tonight or first thing tomorrow."

Jack looked at Jules and Gunther, and smiled. "Tomorrow," he said.

"What?!" Jules asked more than said. "I'll be fine. Right, Gunther?"

"You bet," Gunther replied.

"Tomorrow it is," Buck said, giving Jules and Gunther a sly wink. "Looks like we're not needed here Jack, let's grab a cold one at the bar."

Late Saturday morning, Jules waltzed into Anna's kitchen with an added hop to her step. Anna looked at her, and smiled.

"What?" Jules asked. She was sure that Anna knew about her and Gunther's midnight cruise on the Hunter. And even though Big John was their chaperone, he would be conveniently occupied with Kala.

"You got mail," Anna said, and motioned to a letter on the table.

"Who's it from?"

"Does a return address from Huntsville, Texas ring any bells?"

Jules grabbed the letter, smiling while she ripped it open.

"Vat does it say?" Anna asked.

"It says I better be at the Karolyi ranch on June 27th for a five day, elite camp session. And that I better be in shape if I want to go to the World Championships in Stuttgart come December."

The end

Acknowledgements

As with each of my accomplishments in life I have quite a few people to thank and acknowledge.

I would have never attempted writing—period—if not for my wife Donna Esna Hilgreen—rest in peace. To my son James, my daughter Jacqueline, and my granddaughter Jules—love you always.

Special thanks go to my mentor Dr. Lyn Alexander, a godsend who showed me the tools, and worked tirelessly to help me become a writer. I also thank my editors, Joyce Shaughnessy, Robert Tozer, and my sister Gen Hilgreen. And to my graphic artists who designed the beautiful cover of First Of Jules, Nancy Batra and my niece Jamee Mascia—thank you.

To my fellow authors and writing friends from the Writers 750 Group who constantly inspire me and offered bits of wisdom—thank you all.

Lastly to the following friends who made a positive impact on my life; wherever God finds you, I hope you appreciate the use of your names as characters in the novel: Michael "Jessy" Jesberger, Roy Singh, Jai Singh, Jack Mameli, Jerry Smith, Greg Correa, Big John, Bob Brennan, Ron "Sarge" Porter, Charles Snowdan Jones, James "Whitecloud" White, Ronny "Priest" Crowe, Bob "Gunny" Denis, and Micky "Don Hoffman" Livingston.

Jules is back in

SECOND

CHANCES

A cipher, encrypted on the symbol of a secret society reveals clues of the death of an inner circle member of The Corporation.

Jules is on her way to Huntsville, Texas for a week of intense training with Team USA.

The only granddaughter of the recently deceased former President of the Peoples Republic of China is on the war path, and Jules Spenser is on her list.

To make matters worse, Dr. Bryce Kellogg is not happy with her detainment and wants revenge.

For an excerpt—
Turn the page

Her cobalt blue eyes lit up when she spotted Buck at the control panel. As she zeroed in, her gait had a matchless step like a ninja riding the wind—true and smooth. Her blonde French braid she wore to the middle of her back never moved.

As she kissed her Grandpa on the cheek, she lifted the coded letter from the desk. "Buck what is this?" Never one to mince words—Jules had called her grandpa, Buck since she was thirteen and in her mind smarter than him.

"It's a double transposition cipher," he said. "But I'm starting to think there are two frequency shifts."

Jules looked at the crossbones; her eidetic mind already spinning. "Buck, look at the picture. The bones cross. Try a reverse shift on the second key."

Buck stole a quick glance at Jules; made a smirk, and went back to work on the cipher.

"Never mind," Jules said. "I did it in my head. The second key is VOLKAN."

Coming Spring of 2016